T4-APR-555

Gr $8.98
            Greene, Robert Lee
               Haversack and hog
            rifle

DATE DUE

MY 9'92		
MY 15'92		
JE 25'92		
JY 29'92		
AG 14'92		
OC 4'93		
FEB 4 '00		
MY 10 '13		
FE 13 '23		

EAU CLAIRE DISTRICT LIBRARY

DEMCO

HAVERSACK & HOG RIFLE

Robert Lee Greene

TO SOW THE FALLOW SOIL

Winston-Derek Publishers, Inc.
Pennywell Drive—P.O. Box 90883
Nashville, TN 37209

89187
EAU CLAIRE DISTRICT LIBRARY

Copyright 1992 by Winston-Derek Publishers, Inc.

All rights reserved. No part of this book may be reproduced in any form without written permission from the publishers, except by a reviewer who may quote brief passages in a review to be printed in a newspaper or magazine.

First Printing

PUBLISHED BY WINSTON-DEREK PUBLISHERS, INC.
Nashville, Tennessee 37205

Library of Congress Catalog Card No: 89-51632
ISBN: 1-55523- 287-6

Printed in the United States of America

To my mother and father—
Helen and Claude Greene

4/23/92 Donation # 8.⁹⁸

PREFACE

My great-grandfather was born, lived, and died in the mountains of western North Carolina, and is buried on a windswept hill in Watauga County. I always have a feeling of sadness when I try to decipher the few visible initials time has left on the fieldstone markers there, and that is the *why* of this narrative. A grandfather's story should not be forgotten, but passed on generation to generation.

The characters herein were all real people, and the military events, including my great-grandfather's part in them, are true, except where I added thoughts and feelings and certain small details that must be read as fiction. Even those are drawn from the records left by common solders of the time and place, and can be ascribed to Alford without much stretching of the truth.

I chose his friends from the most likely, though no evidence supports it. Silas and Carroll were first cousins and near neighbors, and George Patrick, it is recorded, was a "great pet" to all his comrades.

The people and incidents "at home" are also true, but less is known about his relationships with them, and therefore the narrative is stretched a little more. All of the characters' actions are in keeping with their recorded history, and my great-grandfather *was* there at the time, so it easily *could* have happened like this.

Author's Note

The dialect should not be immediately dismissed as poor or low-class English. It is, rather, a holdover of vocabulary, pronunciation, and syntax of earlier times when it was accepted as good usage. For example, the use of more than one negative, while frowned on today, was widely used by Chaucer and others.

The chapter titles are a bit of doggerel that was popular among the soldiers near the end of the war.

The directional arrows appearing on the maps indicate the position of Alford's regiment in correlation with the text.

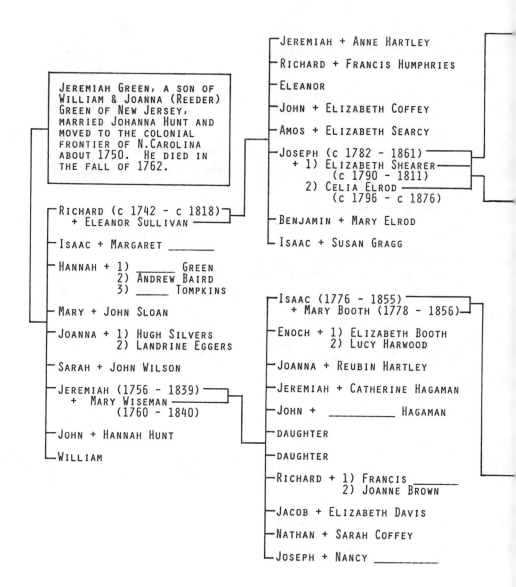

JEREMIAH GREEN, A SON OF WILLIAM & JOANNA (REEDER) GREEN OF NEW JERSEY, MARRIED JOHANNA HUNT AND MOVED TO THE COLONIAL FRONTIER OF N.CAROLINA ABOUT 1750. HE DIED IN THE FALL OF 1762.

RICHARD (c 1742 - c 1818)
    + ELEANOR SULLIVAN ———

ISAAC + MARGARET _____

HANNAH + 1) _____ GREEN
         2) ANDREW BAIRD
         3) _____ TOMPKINS

MARY + JOHN SLOAN

JOANNA + 1) HUGH SILVERS
          2) LANDRINE EGGERS

SARAH + JOHN WILSON

JEREMIAH (1756 - 1839) ———
    + MARY WISEMAN ———
          (1760 - 1840)

JOHN + HANNAH HUNT

WILLIAM

JEREMIAH + ANNE HARTLEY

RICHARD + FRANCIS HUMPHRIES

ELEANOR

JOHN + ELIZABETH COFFEY

AMOS + ELIZABETH SEARCY

JOSEPH (c 1782 - 1861) ———
    + 1) ELIZABETH SHEARER ———
          (c 1790 - 1811)
      2) CELIA ELROD ———
          (c 1796 - c 1876)

BENJAMIN + MARY ELROD

ISAAC + SUSAN GRAGG

ISAAC (1776 - 1855) ———
    + MARY BOOTH (1778 - 1856)

ENOCH + 1) ELIZABETH BOOTH
          2) LUCY HARWOOD

JOANNA + REUBIN HARTLEY

JEREMIAH + CATHERINE HAGAMAN

JOHN + _____ HAGAMAN

DAUGHTER

DAUGHTER

RICHARD + 1) FRANCIS _____
           2) JOANNE BROWN

JACOB + ELIZABETH DAVIS

NATHAN + SARAH COFFEY

JOSEPH + NANCY _____

GREEN
FAMILY
TREE

─ SARAH + RANSOM HAYES

─ ROBERT + 1) CHANIE ELROD
          2) JULIA MOORE

─ ADAM + REBECCA ADAMS

─ MARGARET (1818 - 1886) ────────┐
   + JEREMIAH GREEN   │
                                  │   ┌─ MARY (1840 - 1908)
─ ISAAC + 1) MARY McCANLESS   │   │   + 1) ALFRED CORNELL
          2) SUSAN GRAGG MOORE   │   │   2) JOHN CRISP
                                  │   │
─ AMOS + JULIA McCANLESS   │   ├─ ADAM (1842 - 1863)
                                  │   │   + ANN VANNOY
─ HIRAM + NANCY BROOKSHIRE   │   │
                                  │   ├─ ALFORD (1844 - 1899)
─ DAVID + CATHERINE SMITH   │   │   + HETTIE NORRIS
                                  │   │   (1845 - 1890)
─ MARY + DAVID C. McCANLESS   │   │
                                  │   ├─ ISAAC (1846 - 1885)
─ JOSEPH WARREN + LOUISA MOODY   │   │   + ELIZABETH CORNELL
                                  │   │
                                  │   ├─ SARAH (1848 - 1925)
                                  │   │   + 1) GEORGE HAYES
                                  │   │   2) ISAAC NORRIS
─ ELIZABETH + JONATHAN NORRIS ────┤   │
                                  │   ├─ JOSEPH (1850 - 1880)
─ RACHEL   │   │   + LUCY JANE ADAMS
                                  │   │
─ MARY + SQUIRE ADAMS   │   ├─ ALLEN (1852 - 1925)
                                  │   │   + 1) MARY JANE ADAMS
─ SOLOMON + 1) NANCY HODGES   │   │   2) AMANDA GOODMAN
           2) MARY SHERRIL   │   │
                                  │   ├─ RANSOM (1855 - 1857)
─ JOHN + MARY ESTES   │   │
                                  │   ├─ CELIA (1857 - 1883)
─ ISAAC + SARAH ESTES   │   │   + ADAM E. JONES
                                  │   │
─ DAVID + MARY LOWRANCE   │   ├─ ELIZA (1859 - 1911)
                                  │   │   + EMMETT STANBERRY
─ MARGARET + ALLEN ADAMS   │   │
                                  │   └─ LEANDER (1862 - 1942)
─ NANCY + SAMUEL LOWRANCE   │   + CHANIE CLAWSON
                                  │
─ JEREMIAH (1816 - 1890) ─────────┘
   + MARGARET GREEN

─ SQUIRE + 1) "FANNY" McBRIDE
           2) MARGARET GREEN
              NORRIS

"The generation that carried on the war has been set apart by the experience. Through our great fortune, in our youths our hearts were touched with fire. It was given to us to learn at the outset that life is a profound and passionate thing."

—Oliver Wendell Holmes, Jr.
Memorial Day, 1884

Sixty-one, Had a Lot of Fun

25 January 1899

Folkses call me "old Alf," and there ain't no wonder in it atall. Hell, I'm jes fifty-four and m'hair is still mostly brown, but look at me, with this fusty faded Carolina Lily quilt snugglin' me in the high-back rocker aside the fire, stretchin' time a-readin' my old letters when I orta be out in the barn with the boys. Don't recollect how many years ago the paralysis struck down m'legs and took all a m'strength—"apoplexy," that's what young Doc Hodges called it.

I war tough and able onest, built this double fireplace, and with Paw learnin' me to shape the logs and make lap joints, I put up the whole house. The same oak shingles we cut back then is still in place, tho' many a them is curled up aginst the weather. Should be some repairs made come a nice day. I reckon I learnt most ever'thing I knowed from Paw.

He give me the land, too, eighty acres, but not much of it is left no more since I sold some to Henry Miller and Frank Brown when money was scarce, and then the sheriff sold several more acres on account a what I owed to John Norris' Dry Goods store. Ain't seed a lotsa money in my whole life. The most I ever had at one time was confederate bills, and they soon turned bad. Uncle Allen Adams even papered one side of his living room with his.

What little worldly goods I have left now Henry and Hardy can have, providin' I can live out my days in m'own house. Them boys has been good to me. I remember the summer afore last when they fetched me acrost the branch, through the woodlot with the blackberries a-tearin' at me, and up to the meadow where I could see afar off. I stayed fer hours jes a-lookin' at Howard's Knob and miles all surround. It was a pleasure to be outa this chair.

I would like to go there agin, or take some roses and oxeye daisies yonder to the buryin' ground, but I might not. Some a these days I'll be where I won't have to set no more.

* * *

Camp Fisher
High Point, North Carolina
17 November 1861

Dear Hettie,

The good marchin' order we had when we left Boone was all broke up afore we war past the Green Settlement near the blowing rock, where Maw was borned. The road was steep and there was jes too many of us to keep up any straight lines. Captain Farthing had ever'body a singin' and that helped awhile, but he had to give it up. Then William Shull and Isaac Wilson, who we chose for second and third Lieutenants, jawed at us till somebody hollered for them to shut up or come the next election we would turn them out.

We stopped at Lenoir fer some water and a rest. I reckon the whole town was on the road to cheer us, and even some a the girls from Davenport Womans College was there. They all wore white dresses and straw hats, and we teased them with hoots and whistles cause they warn't allowed to talk with no men. Finally some fellow, a preacher I think, come and shooed them all away whilst we hooted some more. Then we was ordered up and marched off. We kep' our ranks good agin till we was outa town.

2

We had but one more rest afore we got to Speagle's Turnout, the end a the railroad. There was a train a-waitin' fer us and I wisht you was there, cause it ain't nothin' like no picture you ever seed.

It was a machine I can hardly describe. A powerful big smoke stack like a funnel was on the top, and aside it was a beautiful bright polished bell. On the front was a thing called a cow catcher to keep the tracks clear.

It jes sat there all shiny and a-puffin' kinda quiet-like. We was all crowded on the platform fer a close look when all a sudden it made a loud noise and fired steam at us like a dragon, and we all jumped back lest it swallowed us up! I landed on my rear end and took a couple other boys down with me.

When we crammed into the cars and the train snorted and jerked off, I knew the fun had started. It was a rickety bump ride all the way and it shore littered my innards. We went through Statesville and Salisbury where lotsa people stood and hurrahed and waved at us.

When we got off at High Point and marched into Camp Fisher we kep' our order good cause there was soldiers in uniform ever'where a-watchin' us come in. I was surprised there was so many tents and little shanties, jes row after row, hundreds a them, and it was all mud ever which way.

First off we was assigned our tents and handed some equipment. I already brung a lot from home but we had to have the regulation stuff. So I got what they call a forage cap and a gray jacket with brass buttons, some white cotton drawers that don't fit me nohow, a white cloth haversack, a canteen, and a old flintlock musket jes like the one Grandpaw owned.

Then I got a flannel shirt and two blankets. I shoulda got trousers and boots too, but the quartermaster ran out so I have to wait. It all weighs near thirty pounds, and I have to march with it!

My cousins Carroll and Silas, Uncle Squire Green's boys, are in the same tent with me. We was hopin' right from the start that we would stay together.

3

Well, it's nigh unto dark so I will close this letter now, but I will write agin tomorrow.

Your affectionate friend,
Alf

* * *

When I turned seventeen all I thought 'bout was war, and it was all Carroll and Silas and me talked on after we saw the handbill tacked up at Moretz' grist mill down the creek: "One Hundred Men Wanted For A Company Of State Troops. Recruits Will Be Enlisted At Boone On September 18, 1861 By William Young Farthing."

The whole neighborhood was in a debate cause there was as many agin' the war as favored it. M'own brother Adam said North Carolina had no business a-goin' in, fer it would tear the country up. He was agin' it all the way.

But Silas said iffen we don't fight the slaves would rise up and take over the land and use white women fer their wives. I wondered from where he got that! The onliest niggers we ever seed was the two owned by Jesse Mullins over on the South Fork, and then they was stoled off by somebody to be sold in South Carolina.

Paw said, "I was a Union man, but when they sent soldiers south it changed my notion." That was good enough fer me. I was determined to go. "Son, you need not be in sech a hurry to join the army, you are only a boy yet," he said. "But I won't stand in your way."

When I come to the front a the line after Carroll and Silas, I wrote it jes as plain as I could: *Alford Green, Age 17, Height 5' 10 1/2", Weight 158 pounds.*

Watauga Minute Men Enlisted 18 September 1861

William Young Farthing, organizer and appointed Captain
Paul Farthing, appointed 1st Lieutenant
William F. Shull, elected 2nd Lieutenant
Isaac Wilson, elected 3rd Lieutenant

Baird, Andrew
Bingham, Harvey
Blair, William T.
Brewer, David E.
Brewer, James
Cable, Alexander
Cable, George W.
Calloway, William H.*
Clark, Francis M.
Clark, Samuel C.
Coffey, Cornelius J.
Coffey, Joseph D.
Coffey, Thomas N.
Danner, Frederick
Dotson, Abner C.
Dugger, David C.
Eggers, Johiel S.
Farthing, Henry H.
Farthing, James M.
Farthing, John S.
Farthing, John Y.
Farthing, Linley W.
Farthing, Robert H.
Farthing, Thomas J.
Flannery, Joseph D.
Ford, Ephraim W.
Green, Alford
Green, Brazilla C.
Green, Burzilla
Green, Silas
Green, William
Harmon, Cicero D.
Hartley, Bartlett
Hartley, Jonathon H.
Hartley, William
Henson, James
Hilliard, Bartlett Y.*
Hilliard, George W.
Hilliard, Harrison H.
Hilliard, James R.
Hodges, Burton

Howington, Joseph H.
Johnson, Riley
Knight, Levi H.
Lawrence, George W.
Love, James
Moody, Golston
Moody, Hedges*
Munday, James W.
Orrant, Lewis
Patrick, George W.
Phillips, Jordan B.
Pilkinton, Henry A.
Presnell, Elisha L.
Price, Calvin
Price, John
Ricks, George M.C.
Shell, William J.
Shull, Joseph C.
Shull, Nathaniel C.
Shull, Philip P.
Shull, Simon P.
Smith, Abner
Smith, Bennett
Smith, Henry
South, Britton
Stevens, Thomas
Strickland, William
Swift, Dudly
Swift, Samuel
Swift, Sherman
Swift, Young
Teaster, J. harrison
Teaster, Samuel
Trivett, John E.
Ward, Johm
Williams, Thomas R.
Wilson, Albert P.
Wilson, Hiram
Wilson, William C.
Younce, George
Younce, Jacob

*rejected

North Carolina and Watauga County

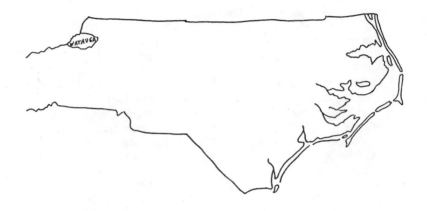

Townships as they were during the Civil War

Camp Fisher
High Point, North Carolina
18 November 1861

Dear Hettie,

We been so busy hereat that I fear the war will be over afore I git to it. We tag up and down these roads near fifty mile every day and don't go nowheres 'cept *forward to the rear, right oblique, left oblique,* and law, the sergeant is ill as a hornet. I don't allow he could teach a dog to bark. When this war is done I am a-gonna whup anyone who says *fall in* to me.

Now I will tell you somethin' about our company. It's called the Watauga Minute Men and eighty-five a the fightinest boys and the straightest shooters there ever was is in it, not counting Captain Farthing. I am the youngest one and Fred Danner is the oldest. He is near fifty years old and I don't know how he got in cause the limit is thirty-four. They don't always go by the rules I reckon, cause on the low end you should be eighteen, but I got in anyhow.

Our tent is a big round one called a Sibley. Twelve of us are in it and we lay in a circle with our feet towards the stove. It's a sight bad on a hot and rainy night I tell you, and I was put by the flap so I git tromped whenever anybody comes or goes!

The food eats good I reckon. Ain't been a-going hungry nohow, but I shore would ruther be a-settin at Maw's table.

I am having lotsa fun tho' with Carroll and Silas and old George Patrick. Did you ever hear tell a him? He is from Laurel Creek, short and as wide as he is long, with a face as red as a turkey snout and a grin from here to there. He tickles me the best ever and I laugh at somethin' old George does every day. Jes last night somebody loaded the firewood with blastin' powder and caused a main ruction. We was all convinced 'twas George who done it, but he won't own up.

I received a letter from Paw. Isaac wrote it fer him, an it was a-waitin' here afore we even come to camp. Says he is proud a me, but brother Adam don't want to join the army and some folkses think anybody who don't join is a coward. Well shoot, Adam ain't no such thing nohow even

7

tho' we always are on the opposite side a every fence. And I don't care iffen he is older than me, Paw needs him to home. As fer me, I jes up and done it.

You know, Adam and me had us a good cuss fight ever now and then but still we was close, and we had some good times too. Not many days but what we warn't a-cuttin' up.

I recollect one time we was jes projectin' around, and we uncovered some popskull in a stump. 'Twarn't long we was both drunk as boiled owls. Then there was the time, and we was old enough to knowed better, that we chewed down about half the sorghum patch. Paw most pointedly flailed hell outa us fer that one. He has a mean temper, and we knowed it, but we was rogues anyhow.

Now, Maw was never mean. Never laid a lick on us. Course we jes loved Maw! Well, I do remember she was powerful tetchus the time we tromped molasses into the house. But that was Uncle Squire's fault. He said, "It's a good thing to put molasses on your feet, it keeps the flies offen your face." So we had to try it! Silas still calls me 'lasses foot over that one. I reckon we all miss the old times, don't we?

You remember that big muster in Boone a month back afore we left? After the drilling was over ever'one was a-cuttin' up. I can see it yet, Colonel Joe Todd, the court clerk, standing in the courthouse door, a-wavin' his sword to prevent Sheriff McBride and his gang from riding their horses right inside the place. And the day we marched off with Captain Farthing. Warn't that every bit like a Fourth a July picnic with so much music and singin' and shoutin'?

You was so pretty with your new dress and the ribbon in your hair. And the little flag you made fer me, I keep it in my sack all the time.

Well, I will close fer now. Give my best respects to your Maw and little brother Jake. Tell him I will fetch him a Yankee hat when I come home.

> Your affectionate friend,
> Alf

* * *

The mind is a queer thing, ain't' it? Some days I cain't name all my children, yet I still hold a picture fer over thirty-five years a sweet Hettie, a-standin' in front a the courthouse with the mud up to her socks, waving good-bye to me.

I knowed her 'bout a year then, cause she lived right nigh Uncle Sam Lowrance, on the Cove Creek side a the mountain. Moved there with her Maw and brother from over in Tennessee after her Paw, Jake Norris, died.

But I reckon that was the day I knowed I loved her.

✳ ✳ ✳

Camp Fisher
High Point, North Carolina
24 December 1861

Dear Hettie,

Captain Farthing says a sight a Yankees are done nigh the sea coast. We might see some fightin' at last, and I won't mind it a bit more than spit in the fire, cause this camp life is boring, boring, boring! And it's filled with the most swearin', and fightin', and drunkeness, and card playin' a body could ever see. Poker, ucher and keno. I joined this army fer some adventure but I ain't got it yet, and iffen I stay a soldier long enough I will be as bad as the worst.

Now it ain't hard, mind you. We answer the roll call and stand guard duty onest in a while and drill over and over agin. We clean the camp, chop wood, and dig trenches, and all of it on a schedule. But I coulda done all that work to home. What I want is to fight a war.

There is many boys that has died from the measles and mumps and newmonie fever. I allow we bury one or two nearly ever' day. Seems like there is as many grave markers as tents in the camp. Jes in our company San Teaster and Henry Pilkinton and Riley Johnson is dead. Words don't come to express the sadness of it, specially when a father or some kin comes to the camp with a box on a wagon to pick up the body so it can be buried at their home place. I was feelin' poorly awhile too and scared some disease was commencin', but I am 'bout like common now. 'Cept this evening I am a little homesick 'cause tomorrow is Christmas.

9

I wonder if there is snow in the mountains. There is jes a little skift on the ground here. It's the prettiest sight in the world when the snow is knee deep in the hollers and shapin' the trees. I wisht I was fishin' Howard's Creek in the snow right now. I would eat every bit a trout I could catch.

I reckon Paw has lit up the wet old hickory Yule log by now, and Maw has commenced to parch the popcorn. The mountains may be rough and rugged, but it's a sweet home to me.

Carroll and Silas is gonna git some music up so I will join them in a minute, but first I want to tell you that I got a letter from brother Adam. He has been sparkin' Ann Vannoy and now he give out the news they is a-gonna get married. Ain't that good to hear?

I wisht you knowed how to write, but iffen you want to send anything, direct it to Company E, Thirty-seventh Regiment, North Carolina Troops. That's what they call us now, Company E, but I still say we are the Minute Men.

Your affectionate friend,
Alf

Sixty-two, Had A Lot to Do

Let me think, it was near the first a January when we moved to
Camp Mangum over nigh Raleigh. Rode on a train, number 101,
and when it would go slow some a the boys hopped off and stole
kisses from the girls a-wavin' at us. I can still see Silas jumpin'
outa the car. "I'm a-gonna' git me that little one with the yeller
hair." Heck, he no sooner hit the ground but the train started up
agin, so he grabbed a peck at her and come runnin', fightin' to
keep his cap on his head. He like to fell under the train iffen we
hadn't pulled him in. "Thank you boys! Thank you Lord!" I
thought my sides would split.

We met General Martin, the inspector general, at Mangum.
Ever'body shore cussed that man out after he ordered us to cut
down on our baggage. He thought one blanket enough, tho' the
trees was bent down with ice and we near friz to death at night.
But we was only there a short time afore we moved to New Berne
'cause the Yankees was makin' a threat to the railhead there.

We camped in the fairgrounds a few days and then moved
acrost the Neuse river and set up Camp Tadpole, a wet, wet place.
It was 'bout two mile from New Berne. We got plenty a fish and
sweet taters and I saw the hardest knock fight a my life there. Two
men argued fer several days, then finally the captain ordered

them to go at it but use only their fists. Nobody was to interfere till one or t'other hollered "enough."

After a long fight the captain thought best to call a halt. I opine both a them would have died ruther than sing out "enough."

A little after that we moved to Camp Lee, below New Berne.

* * *

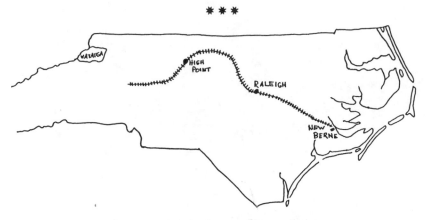

Part of the North Carolina Railroad in 1861

Camp Lee
New Berne, North Carolina
9 March 1862

Dear Hettie,

We are 'specting a fight any time now, and I have to confess to mortal fear a the battlefield. It shore uneasies me, and I pray that strength will be given to stand and do my duty. They was a preacher come this mornin', 'cause it's the Sabbath, and he made us a little speech. "Boys, you need to never fear to trust the Lord." Law, I pray so! Me and Carroll and Silas made us a pact that iffen anyone was kilt, the others would not let the Yankees git to the body, but would see it was buried decent. Then we put our hands on Silas' Testament and swore on it.

Our breastworks, made outa logs and earth, is finished. It run more than two mile betwixt Fort Thompson and Brice Creek. We set into diggin' 'bout two weeks ago after Roanoke Island fell to the Federals, 'cause General Branch says they are a-comin' here next. I am plumb wore out from the job. Four thousand a us soldiers is here but we ain't had the necessaries to work with 'cept old worn shovels and axes. The general advertised in all the papers fer tools and men, but there was onliest a few come in. I can at least rejoice to God fer giving me good strength.

Captain Farthing says the enemy will be a-comin' up the river. Most a our guns are set thataway, and we planted the river with torpedoes. Shoot! Waitin' must be hard as fightin'. It is a thousand wonders that I sleep atall. Sometimes in the night I hear a little racket and it jes undoes me.

Farewell fer awhile,
Alf

* * *

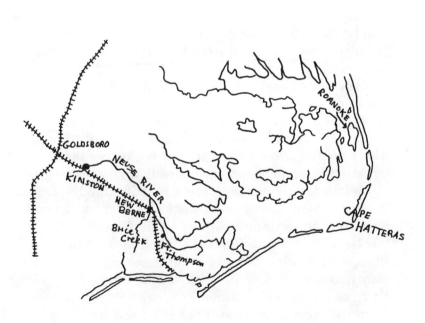

13

EAU CLAIRE DISTRICT LIBRARY

Kinston, North Carolina
17 March 1862

Dear Hettie,

It was three o'clock in the mornin' Thursday when we was shook outa our tents and ordered into battle gear. We had no time to think on lost sleep, and was marched into position to the left a the old Beaufort Road.

We waited there all day an my skin was jes crawlin' all over me, but the Yankees stayed on their boats. I tried to git some rest but every time I shut my eyes a two hundred pounder from a gunboat sailed over me. Long 'bout sundown it came a hard rain and the Yanks snuck onto land and set up camp fer the night no more than two mile from us. Then Captain Farthing give us a speech.

He told us not to shoot till we are in close range, and if possible, to pick off the officers. He said we are less apt to be kilt a-goin' forward than if we retreat, and not to stop to plunder the dead, or heed the calls of wounded comrades, fer the best way to protect our friends is to drive the enemy from the field. Then he warned us that cowards will be shot! He told us all that 'cause it was our first fight. All night long I weighed what the Captain said aginst the pact Silas and Carroll and me made.

Then 'bout daylight, from the woods in front a us, the Yanks come on, shootin' through a shut-down fog, nine regiments to five a ours. My heart was a-poundin' and my hands shook so bad I worried that I could load the gun. The very first time I fired it off I hollered as loud as I could, and then I hollered every breath till we stopped.

Jes afore twelve o'clock we was ordered to the right a the road to aid the Seventh Regiment. We had to move four hundred yards under heavy artillery fire.

Now, there was a railroad crossed at the center a our lines, with a brickyard and a kiln next to the track. The only troops we had in the brickyard was some green militia from around this county. They was only in the army 'bout two weeks. Anyhow, the steady fire a muskets crackled fer near to three hours. Then the Yanks stormed on that

14

brickyard and those new militia boys broke and took off like scalded dogs. By the time we knowed it, it was too late, fer we was outflanked and short a ammunition.

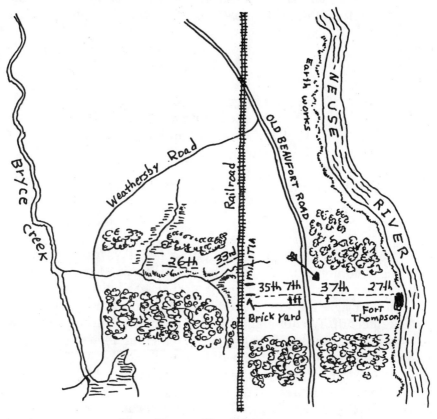

New Berne Battlefield

The order to retreat come down and every man struck out as fast as he could, and some ran the whole five miles to New Berne where a train was jes pullin' out. Some a them scrambled onto that train and I reckon they is still a-goin'.

'Bout four hundred soldiers was counted missing and the Captain reckons half a them was on the train. The rest of us fell back in good order to Kinston, where we are now, breathin' a spell. Every man in our company come through the fight so far as I can tell. I am jes happy to be alive.

15

All the troops ain't arrived in camp yet, and them that made it is all outa sorts and hungry enough to eat army mules.

You will shorely hear all 'bout the big Yankee victory, but don't think ill of us. I reckon we will git even.

Your friend always,
Alf

"I can't forget one look of thine
Though miles apart we be,
While life shall last and memory reign
I will remember thee."

I copied that from a book.

* * *

Our spirits was up agin in only a few days 'cause fresh troops kep' a-comin' in till we had about five thousand men.

Iffen my memory serves right, that was when we was formed into a brigade under General L. O'Bryan Branch. The Seventh, Eighteenth, Twenty-eighth, Thirty-third and Thirty -seventh Regiments was put together, and we had a grand review in Kinston fer the generals and all a the people in the town.

Kinston. I can't think a that place withouten I think 'bout Keith Blalock. And I have to laugh ever' time.

I recall it was Silas who woked me up in the middle a the night when he come off guard duty to tell me the whole story of it. I can hear him yet! "Alf, wake up, you gotta hear this." He shook me so hard I grabbed m'pants 'cause I thought the Yanks was comin'. "No, be still and listen," he said, "Do you know Keith Blalock who lives under Grandfather Mountain, not too far off from your Uncle Robert Green's place?"

M'eyes was still half shut but Silas was a-talkin' fast now. "Well, last month 'bout a week after the battle, Keith come in and joined the Twenty-sixth, and damned iffen he didn't fetch his own wife, Malinda Sarah, right along with him. She warn't 'bout to be left behind so she cut her hair and told the enlister that she was his brother Sam! So they took her in and she wore a uniform, and toted a high-power, and tented and messed with Keith, jes like a reg'lar soldier, right here at Kinston! Ain't that one more sight?"

I nodded and was 'bout to tell Silas to slow down with his story when the man in the next cot broke in. "She's here? With us?" Silas moved around betwixt us and stepped it up a little louder. "And whilst ourn regiment was a bathin' in the river last week Malinda clum up on the bank to take a gander. Oh, boys, don't you wisht we'd a-knowed it then?"

Now I was wide awake, and Silas' audience was a-growin'. "But Keith, her husband and partner, now he jes had no use fer the army, least not ours, and there's some a the men say he'd be right happy on the Union side, but I don't know. Anyway, he aimed to git home somehow or 'nother, so a while ago he went a-wallerin' in some poison oak. The surgeon thought he musta' had some unknown contagion 'cause he was given a medical discharge."

Now the whole tent was awake and in a roar, 'specially tryin' to recall what fool games we was a-playin' in the river whilst Malinda watched us. But Silas kep' the story goin'. "Now what's Malindy Sary Sam a-gonna' do in the army by herself? Well, she fessed up, that's what, and the General, after seein' he was really a she, discharged her right quick! She jes left the camp today."

Silas shore was pleased how his news went over so good, and it did, 'cause we joked and talked on the Blalocks long after we left Kinston. Years later I heared that it warn't no time till Keith was a-settin' in some brine at home and got hisself shed a the poison. Then they tried to arrest him and send him back to the army but he lit out fer the Grandfather afore they got to him. He was a home Yankee all the way.

We all left Kinston not long after Malinda did, early in May it was. Hurried off to Virginia 'cause the Yankees had unloaded a huge army off from four hundred ships onto the peninsula, and our general was afeared they would attack Richmond.

❋ ❋ ❋

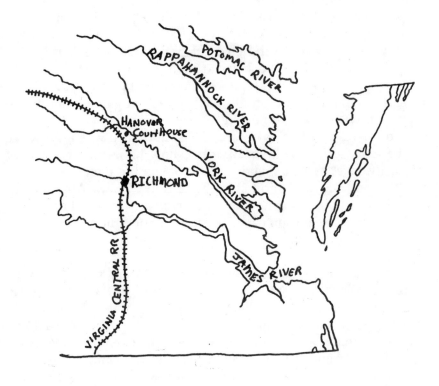

Hanover Court House, Virginia
18 May 1862

Dear Maw and Paw,
   When we left North Carolina we went to Gordonsville
and stayed a few days, then we was ordered to join General Jackson in the Shenandoah Valley. We marched fer two
days to the base of the Blue Ridge when orders come to go
back. So! We countermarched and tromped back to Gordonsville, and then some more orders come, and we
dogged our way from there to here. Shoot! Seems like the

18

generals cain't make up their minds wuther to lick or spit. We are now 'bout eighteen mile north a Richmond, not far from Hanover Court House.

About twenty green-as-grass recruits has joined the company, and that makes 'bout one hundred men now, 'cept several more died from the fever. Most all a the new boys is from Watauga.

We have enlisted fer two more years. Now, I can jes see Maw a-carryin' on. Well, I knowed it's a cruel war but I have to do my duty. Besides, I warn't a-gonna' be the only man to decline. Heck. I wisht some a them idlers back home crossin' over into Tennessee to avoid conscription would have to do some marchin' and diggin' here, too. But I reckon we ain't got a bit a use fer them no way, as that kind would do more harm than help.

Paw, you say Adam might be taken by the conscript. Well, I heared say a family can send a younger man as a substitute fer one needed to home, and he and Ann is married now, but I jes don't know the whole law on it. I cain't tell him or nobody else what to do, but I will say there is no fun bein' a soldier like I thought.

Tell him iffen he does join it would be worse to come here than to go to camp somewheres in the mountains, fer more die here from disease than from guns.

Give howdy to all my brothers and sisters and tell them to write to me.

Your faithful son,
Alf

＊ ＊ ＊

Castle Williams
Governor's Island
New York Harbor, New York
18 June 1862

Dear Maw and Paw,

It ain't easy to tell you what a bad fix I am in now, but I have to do it 'cause I might never see you no more. I been dragged all the way to New York, to a Yankee prison that sets on a island in the bay. It's close to the city 'cause I can see a big church acrost the water less than a mile away. We was taken three weeks ago, and it all happened so fast my head twists a-thinkin' on it.

Back on 26 May we was moved to Slash Church to cover the Virginia Central Railroad. The next day we saw a mess a Yankees comin' on to tear up the tracks, so we hid in the woods to wait. Well, three batteries a cannon stormed on our brigade till General Branch tired of it and ordered us to attack.

We raged outa the woods and poured a heavy volley at them and split their line, but they kep' sendin' men in, more and more, 'cause we was up aginst a whole division. It warn't no use to keep on. Under orders from the General we tried to fall back but was soon scurried into a rout.

'Bout five hundred a us was snagged and hauled down the peninsula where we was put on a boat. I tell you, I ain't never been on no boat like that in my life. Afore we rode all the way to this side a the world I was sick as a dog. We landed here on 2 June.

At least I warn't alone. Silas and George Patrick and more than thirty a the company was bagged, too. We was all in need a repairs by the time we wabbled off that boat and into this Yankee fort they use fer a jail. They didn't catch Carroll so he is still with the regiment and safe I reckon, but now the three of us is broke up fer the first time.

Iffen you can, send one a the children to tell Hettie the news. I might can write to her, but now I ain't got no more paper.

We ain't been treated too bad by the Yankees, but the place scares me to death. There is little tents and shacks all over, and a big round brick fort they call Castle Williams where I am. It's like a deep cold dungeon with nothin' in it but hard floors and our bed sacks. Even the guards hate it cause they say it is infested with the smallpox from the inmates that was here before. Gives me nightmares.

Jes the second night here I was woked up by a storm

before the mornin' and raised my head, and there was a rat sittin' on my stomach a-starin' right into my eyes. I nearly crawled up the wall tryin' to git away from it. A body can never feel clean here.

Even the sinks where we do our private things stand right out in the middle a the grounds under the watch a the guards. They are all polluted, too, and we fear it will git into the drinkin' wells afore long.

When I came here the Yanks traded my old clothes fer some clean ones but they ain't clean no more.

The food they give us we fix ourselves on a range in the yard, but the pork is so fat all we can make is greasy water soup. George says we are better off jes to laugh at it and he is right. He claims the soup is too weak to drown the worms in it, but iffen you leave them alone a minute or two they will starve to death. Some a the boys pick up rotten trash on the beach and eat that, too.

The worst of ever'thing is the boredom. It jes never quits. Most a the time I pitch stones or play a checker game or whittle. I carved a little ring outa bone and traded it to a guard fer a stamp and this paper.

Every day I hear they are a-fixin' to make a prisoner exchange, some a us fer some a the Yankees, but they ain't no tellin'. The guards say it's 'cause neither side wants to take the trouble to feed and care fer so many prisoners and they would be better off to trade them back. After awhile I don't believe nothin', tho', and thinkin' on it jes gives me a headache. We are all thataway.

Yesterday I catched a man stealin' my envelope and I near kilt him. I grabbed his hair and banged his head aginst the brick wall till he went out, and then I was a-gonna' stomp him 'cept George stopped me. He and Silas jes shook their heads like I had lost my mind. I am sorry about it now. I reckon there is at least one fight every day. We all stand around and cheer and the guards don't care. They figure if we kill each other off they will have less to do.

I hope this writin' makes it to North Carolina. We are only allowed to make ten lines in a letter, but the guard who give me the paper said he would see that it was posted. He will give it to one a the visitors who come on the island. A few a the prisoners has relatives who live in the North, and they come to visit now and then, and bring food and things, too. None in my company is so fortunate.

Pray fer all of us, that we may see home agin. Two N.C. boys died here already. The last one was buried today.

Your faithful son,
Alf

* * *

Some people will say they would jes love to live on a island away off somewheres, 'cause they admire the freedom. Not fer one day could I stand it!

Oft times it's a little thing that will lay you low, and it was so fer me in the prison. One day when a few of us from the regiment was settin' on our bunks a-talkin' on nothin' in partic'lar, and markin' the days on the calendar we had scratched on the wall, a guard come by.

"We hear you Rebels have a new general now," he said. "The name is Lee, Robert E. Lee. Took over after Johnston was wounded at Seven Pines. Gave your army a new name, he did. Calls it the 'Army of Northern Virginia' now." The words jes fell to the bottom a m' stomach. 'Twas as if we was wrote off forever . . . the Army of *Virginia*. What 'bout me and all the other North Carolina boys? It was silly I know, yet I didn't eat nary a thing fer days, and m'head jes could not talk me back up.

But come 10 July I was a-flyin' agin, 'cause over a thousand of us, all 'cept a few a the very sick, was herded onto a steamer, the Baltic, and that night we saw the last a New York Harbor.

We yakked like schoolchildren off on a sail, all convinced we was on the way to freedom, but we soon hushed when we discovered ourselves unloadin' on Pea Patch Island! This one was in the Delaware River and nothin' was on it 'cept a wall surround some shed barracks. They called it Fort Delaware but it was nothin' but marshy ground to me. It was several feet below the high water level and the dikes they made leaked most a the time.

It was in all ways worse than Governor's Island. Here they searched us several times fer "concealed arms." Instead, they took away every pocket knife that was of value. And whilst we was away from our sheds, they ransacked our clothes and statchels. Any little trinket they found was taken like a trophy. Some guard even bore off a ambrotype of a boy's dead mother that he kept with him through every battle.

One night nineteen prisoners escaped the island. The weather was stormy and kep' the guards under cover, so the men took apart a privy down by the shore and made them a raft.! The bank was covered with thick reeds so they had a easy time of it.

Course that set us all a-thinkin', and me and Silas had a little meeting to see if anybody had some good idea, tho' we knowed it would have to be some difficult thing, fer the guards was now on the alert.

About then the prison commander announced we was all to be traded, and as soon as the boats arrived we would be taken back to Virginia. This time I fought off my hopes and walked 'bout fer two days sayin' to m'self, "Wait fer the boats! Wait fer the boats!" Then it happened.

The very last day a July two steamers come, the Merrimac and the Atlantic, and made ready fer us.

* * *

Richmond, Virginia
7 August 1862

Dear Maw and Paw,

I am free! Day afore yesterday, on Wednesday, a little after noon, we was placed ashore and all a us was traded fer some Yankee prisoners.

We had left Fort Delaware, what we call Starvation Island, on 1 August, early in the mornin', and sailed up the James River to Aiken's Landing, just below the Dutch Gap

Canal. We was under the flag a truce to keep our own boys from firin' on us. It warn't till the fifth that we landed, and I allow my throat was lumped every inch a the way fer fear they wouldn't be enough Yanks to trade fer each a us.

But now I am free, and I feel like a colt with all the sunshine a the world meltin' on me.

Our orders say to report to General Winder fer food and quarters till transportation back to the regiment is made, but law, we are so puny we can't strike a lick, so most of us will get a pass to go home.

I might can git there afore this letter does, but I wrote it anyway, jes in case. Look out the window fer me.

Your faithful son,
Alf

✳ ✳ ✳

Me, George, Silas and a few Beaver Dam boys rode a train car fer partways and then walked the rest. To this day I ain't never took no sweeter walk than that'n.

When I first saw the Blue Ridge I thought it was jes clouds a shiftin' and shapin', but afore long I knowed it was real.

We walked a little faster then, up the twisty road betwixt Wolf Knob and Chestnut Mountain and acrost the top a the Laurel Spur.

Little trickles a water commenced to wander in the mosses and ferns and stones 'neath the laurels and rhodies, and run acrost the road here and there. I thought the smell a the hemlock and ash and ever'thing all along the lane would last me a lifetime. One by one each of us followed a different path through the corn fields, by pretty houses with roses clingin' on them.

When I stopped at the rail fence, it seemed a sight longer ago than one year since me and Adam and Paw laid the criss-cross logs down. Onest I jumped over the fence I knowed I was home.

Paw and Isaac, who was sixteen already, left their scythes a-layin' in the hay and walked acrost the field to the house with me, arm over arm.

24

Sallie, Joe, and Allen, he was nine year old then, came a-scurry with baskets a-swingin' and blackberries makin' a trail behind them. I still see Mary, twenty-two and not married off yet, throwin' handfuls a beans in the air and runnin' with a shout, and kissin' me all over m'face. And little Celia and Eliza leaped from the house and was all over me like lovesick puppies.

Maw was in the doorway a-wipin' the tears with her apron. Aginst her shoulder was Leander, m'new brother who was borned whilst I was in prison. My dear mother— she gave her whole heart to her family.

Oh, we shore had a dinner that day, with chicken and dumplins, souse and sausage, cabbage and corn bread, and taters and chow-chow, and bread and egg custard and peach cobbler. It was a feast fer a king and the king was me.

Fer some several hours that night aside the firelight, I told all the tales 'bout the prison, Keith and Malinda Blalock, an sech. Brother Isaac's eyes growed bigger'n a old owl's, an he couldn't hear enough of it.

The best of all was when Maw hauled out the wash tub, cause it was nigh onto two months since I had a scrubbin', and I hurt to get shed a the prison dirt. I didn't fit the tub as when I was little, but I squatted the best I could and nearly wore ever'body out totin' the hot water.

It was the beatinest homecoming a body could have.

The next mornin' I put on m'army pants and cap, and made a soon start acrost the Rich Mountain to see Hettie. She was pullin' weeds from the cabbage when I come up.

Women shore have a way to twist a man all up. You'd a-thought she'd have a grand welcome, and she did pop up with a big grin at first, but then she commenced to sullen around. I *thought*, that's the crap! , but I *said*,

"What's wrong, Hettie?"

"Nothin."

"Ain't you glad I'm home?"

"I am."

"Well, what then?"

"I don't know, I jes look so torn down in this tacky thing, I reckon."

And on it goes till afore you knowed it, I am a-pamperin' her

25

as iffen 'twas she who was jes back from the war, and ever'thing had to start over from scratch! I hain't figgered women out yet.

Her Maw and Jake did give me a fittin' howdy and a squeeze though, and soon we was a-settin' on the porch with me tellin' the stories agin. Then after a while, Hettie come out with her clothes changed, honin' to take a walk.

We went no place in partic'lar, but wound up in the little Green buryin' ground on the side a the hill alongside Sharp Creek, where m'great-granddad and grandmaw is laid. I found the grave rocks and we traced our fingers over the marks.

J.G. Jeremiah Green, B. Feb 15 1756, D. Dec 31 1839.

M.G. Mary Green, B. Feb 16 1760, D. April 15 1840.

He was a soldier of the Revolution, and Paw was named after him.

We talked on fer near a hour 'bout him, with me a-tellin' 'bout m'great-granddad on Maw's side, Richard Green, who was a pioneer in the mountains and had a wide scope a land, 'bout fifteen hundred acres, way up the middle fork. He was a founder a the first church in the whole county, Three Forks Baptist. Hettie was then a-tellin' 'bout her great-grandfather, Ebeneazor Fairchild, who came from New Jersey with a preacher in October 1757 and kept a diary on the whole trip.

All a sudden a big old pilot snake skedaddled from behind a stone and set us both off like a shot. Hettie went a-runnin' up the hill through a rough and caught her dress and jes ruint it.

I disremember what I said next, but she went to sobbin' and carryin' on so, I didn't know where to turn. Finally I jes grabbed her and kissed her, and I reckon that was the best thing,'cause afore long she melted and we was both a-singin' and skylarkin' down the hill.

We stayed there near the whole day, jes holdin' hands or lyin' in the grass puttin' names on the clouds.

Ever-thing was back like afore.

Things after that jes comes to mind in bits and pieces.

Like the corn shuckin' at Uncle Sam Lowrance's place. Now, nary anythin' was more serene to me on a cold October day than to hunt chestnuts under the leaves, and then top it off with a shuckin' bee at night. And when Uncle Sam gathered the young folkses there gen'rally was a heap more frolickin' than work done, with Aunt Nancy servin' up roasted sweet taters outa the fire-place and makin' over ever'body there. It was a big time, and all the girls and boys paired off all surround a mountain a corn jes south a the barn.

But the shuckin' I remember that year warn't no great party. Fer one thing, it struck me hard how many men was gone, as we had nearly all old folkses and little children there. Withouten Hettie with me, I might not a stayed.

M'aunt and uncle was clever folkses and did ever'thing they could to make us all forget the hard times the war brought, so Hettie and me went along. Pretty soon we was settin' off on the far side, a-shuckin' and a-singin',

Oh, I'm a-goin' to the shuckin',
I'm a-going' to the shuckin' of the corn!

The pile was only down a bit when Silas dipped in unbe-knownst outa the shadows. He was decked out in his uniform from top to bottom and all the girls' tongues commenced a-waggin' like bell clappers. After making respects to Uncle Sam and Aunt Nancy, he come direct to me.

"We'uns need to talk," he said, and I saw by his face it was somethin' big so we stepped over nigh the meat house.

"I'm a-goin' back, Alf. George and some a the others, too. We'uns are leavin' in the mornin' at sunup, and I hoped you war a-comin' too."

M' throat dried out so's it was hard to talk. "I don't know wuther I am ready or not." His face scrunched and he come back quick, "I wouldn't spend an opinion on that, but I hope you ain't a-gonna' tie up with them cowards layin' out all over these moun-tains, are you?"

Afore I could answer, he finished it off. "Alf, I cain't leave Car-roll there by hisself, and iffen you forgot our promise, I ain't. And one more thing, when the conscript officer catches up with you he will haul you back to Virginia anyways, and they will throw you in jail iffen they don't jes shoot you first." He pushed a copy of the *Carolina Watchman* in m'hand and was gone.

I moved closer to the light where I could see and studied the paper. It told about the battles ourn boys was in at Second Manas-sas and Sharpsburg, where the Thirty-seventh arrived jes in time to throw the Yankees back. But General L. O'Bryan Branch was kilt by a bullet through his head. At Shepherdstown, it said, the regiment crost a corn field in the "face of a withering artillery fire and drove the enemy across the Potomac."

I put the paper under a rock, thinkin' I would pick it up later and went back to Hettie. I sat as close as I could and tried to clear m'mind with teasin'.

"Ain't you glad your Maw trusted me with you tonight?" She throwed the stray black hairs off her face and said, "You best git shuckin' or this stack ain't never gonna' end. What did Silas want with you?"

Jes then our hands latched onto the same ear a corn. "Oh, nothin', I reckon," I said, and leant back on m'elbow to pull her hand close. But she pulled it loose, all feisty.

"I s'pose you ain't a-gonna' be 'round here much longer, anyhow." Afore I could answer she was up and kicked off her shoes at me and went off. "I'm a-gonna' get me some water."

I catched up afore she reached the springhouse, and tried to lighten up. "I knowed somethin' better'n that to drink, Hettie."

"What are you talkin' 'bout?"

"Right back here. Look." I shifted a rock from a little pile and pulled out the jug.

"What's that? Corn likker?"

"Yep," I said, "It's Uncle Sam's. I seed'm stash it here."

"Well, you jes put the sorry thing back!"

"Oh, come on, Hettie. One little smidgen ain't a-gonna' do you no harm." I popped the cork and she wheeled into the springhouse, so I tilted the jug onest, put it back, and followed her.

"A'right, I'll be a good boy, but you owe me somethin'."

"What do I owe to you?"

"Well, you knowed what they always say. Iffen you find a red ear a corn, then you git to kiss the girl a your choice."

"You ain't found no red ear!"

"I might have," and I reached in m'pocket and pulled it out. "Now what do you say?"

She laughed out loud and quick covered her mouth with both hands. "Well, I reckon ever'body heared that," she said, a-gigglin' and leanin' on the cold trough. I pressed aginst her slow like, and she give up the finder's reward.

"Alf, I don't want you a-goin' back to that war. Too many boys is gettin' kilt ever'day, and there's somethin' I ain't told you 'cause Momma didn't want you to fret. Some men avoidin' the conscription, a pretty smart gang of 'm too, maybe a dozen, came to our house 'bout two months ago. They wanted meat and taters but Momma told'm we ain't had nothin'. Alf, they pushed her to the ground and went right in the house and jes tore it apart a-lookin'. Jake and me was hid by the log pile but we saw it all. They took ever' little bit a food we had and then smashed up Paw's old chair on the door so's to make Momma tell where there was any more hid away. When she said there was nothin' hid one man slapped her acrost the head. "It's a mean place here now, and I am scared of it."

I considered tryin' to tell her what it means to be absent without leave, but the words was slow to come. Then a fiddle started up a old-timey song and she headed back to the barn. "Iffen you do go, I might not be a-waitin' the next time."

When I got home that night I asked Paw what he thought, and he said it was all up to me and he cain't make up my mind fer me. Maw told me that Paw did need me, but he warn't a-gonna' say so, and as fer her, warn't it enough that her oldest boy was off fightin' somewheres?

So I thought on it some more, and finally let Silas and the boys go withouten me, figurin' there was no sense fightin' fer the low-lander's niggers and eleven dollars a month. Specially the way some men sent in paid subsitutes, a-makin' it a rich man's war and a poor man's fight anyway. I reckon I convinced m'self I was right.

Things was peaceful fer several weeks and Paw and Isaac and me did all the things we done afore the war come. We made molasses, strippin' the sorghum stalks of their blades and then cuttin' them into bundles. Paw would feed them in one side a the mill whilst I grabbed them on t'other, give'm a twist, and hand them back to Paw to send through the crusher agin. Isaac tended the horse round and round to power the grinder. Then we cooked the juice in a big trough under a shed. It was the best ever.

On the shrinking of the moon it came time to kill the hogs. Some say the best time is on a growing moon, but not Paw, or Grandpaw neither. Paw says, "The proof is in the fryin'. If the bacon curls up, you know it was butchered in the light a the

○

29

moon, and meat butchered on the dark a the moon flats out and you git a heap a grease." I always hated my part, which was to hold the hog whilst paw cracked its skull with the flat side of a axe. But I knowed it meant good eatin' later on, with sausage, fresh pork, and liver mush, come the next March after proper curing.

We spent some time preparin' the tools fer the winter, too, and so it went till we went to Blowing Rock and things turned fer me.

The funeral preachin' fer Aunt Chanie took us there, to the Green Settlement, as it was called then. She died 29 November.

When word come, it was too late to get to the settin' up, but Maw was determined not to miss the buryin'. They was all her people over there, Uncle Robert bein' Maw's brother and Aunt Chanie her cousin, so she wanted to take some food and help with the cleanin' after.

Isaac and me sweeped the wagon out and hitched the team. Paw had in mind to trade the year-old heifer fer a spare bed Uncle Robert had, so we tied it on the back, and ever'body clambered on.

About halfway was the middle fork, five miles I reckon, and it was a-risin', so Maw and the younguns and the heifer crost over on the footbridge whilst Paw, Isaac and me muscled the wagon through.

Maw got mad as whiz when Paw stopped to hunt some sang on the shady side of a gully, and we'uns picked us a basket a persimmons that was jes good fer eatin'. But we made it on time.

There was many people met in the graveyard that day fer the buryin', and many I never seed afore. I think some of'm was jes drawn to it 'cause it was a funeral. Some folkses is that way.

I stood near Maw and heared Uncle Robert tell all 'bout Aunt Chanie's passing, whilst they brung her box up on the steer wagon. "The doctor could not do a thing for her, Margaret. I stood over till the very last and I done all I could. Oh, what a sad thing it is to think about. I had her a fine coffin made of the finest of walnut, and I bought her a fine dress so she could be put away as nice as any woman could be put away. She could talk till the very last, then she turned over on her side and was dead in a minute. Never struggled but onest."

Three preachers was there and they all preached, but still it

30

was all over in about three hours. We went back to Uncle Robert's below the Flat Top Mountain, where we stayed the night with a crowd a people.

Next day it was like a family reunion, only all sober-wise, and we catched up on all the news. Most a the talk was on the war and I shied off from it when I could. I was glad when Paw told me to take the wagon and fetch the bed. It was at Uncle Robert's other place down in the Globe Valley, about five miles and acrost the county line.

M'cousin Leander went with me. He was a year younger'n me, and Maw always said he was both m'first cousin and m'second cousin, all dependin' on which way you figure it out, 'tho' I ain't never tried. (Now I heared he died over in Boone two month ago. He shore growed up to be somebody, that boy. Started up the *Enterprise* paper and was a representative at Raleigh awhile, and jes lately was a superior judge.)

Well, we got to the Globe and loaded the bed, and it was a good one with a corded bedstead and straw tick and carved end posts. Uncle Robert claimed he coulda sold it fer eight dollars!

'Twas on the way back when the trouble started.

We had commenced to round a bend in the foothills when we saw two men with white beards and black suits settin' straight as ramrods on their horses in the road. First I thought they was preachers from the funeral, but when we pulled up, I seed that one of'm was Reubin Coffey. I knowed him from somewheres 'cause he was in'law to Maw's sister Sarah. So we stopped the team and both of us gave a respectful howdy.

Then Reubin said, "Howdy to you boys. This is my brother, William Coffey. The Lord shore made a nice day today, did he not?" He looked at Leander. "You are one of Robert's boys, ain't you? How old are you now?"

"I jes turned seventeen, sir," said Lee.

"And you," he was turned straight at me now, "I don't reckon I know your family."

"Yes, sir, you do," I answered. "My Paw is Jeremiah Green from Meat Camp, and my name is Alford."

"Well, that's kinda what we thought. We seen you at the funeral, you know. You was with the Thirty-Seventh Regiment awhile, were you not?" I felt some uneasy the way the questions was a-turnin', but I stayed respectful.

31

"Yes, sir, I was."

"And why are you here now instead of with your own company?"

"Well, sir, I was taken a prisoner by the Yankees and when we was turned loose I came home to—" He threw his hand up to stop me.

"I know that boy, and now you are absent without leave, is that not so?"

I couldn't hide the squirmin' whilst thinkin' of a answer, and then he calmly raised a rifle gun point blank at me and said flat out, "Alford Green, we are taking you under arrest in the name of the conscription officers. Now, git your ass down from the wagon." I did what I was told.

"You," he said to Leander, git on with your own business." Lee shot me a helpless look and started off with Paw's wagon.

Reubin lit from his horse and grabbed a rope offen the saddle. I knowed he had in mind to tether me, so with no thought atall I took a swing at his rifle, knocked it to the ground, and took off like a sore-tailed bear. I saw him scramble fer the gun and afore I reached the edge a the woods a bullet whistled past m'ear and thunked the tree jes as I spun around it.

I kep' a-runnin' and tore up the steep hill through the sorrel toward Flat Top, barkin' m'shins more'n onest! I have no idea how long it took me to git to Uncle Robert's but I was so petered out I had to set on m'hunkers awhile afore I could look over all the horses there to make certain the Coffeys warn't around. Then I hunted up Paw. Lee had already give him the news and he was jes gettin' fixed to come after me. He told me to git to the wagon quick, and then he fetched the whole family out.

After proper farewells, at least as proper as could be at sech a time, we headed fer home. I had nothin' to say all the way, and I cain't say iffen I was more mad or fearful.

Fer some several weeks after I was always on the watch fer the conscripter or anybody else a-comin' unbeknownst. I was even afeared to visit Hettie withouten it was in the night, and then I never did stay long. Christmas come and went and I don't recollect nothin' of it.

As time went on it seemed like I growed as mean as a black snake. I was hatin' ever'thing and ever'body, and myself the most. One warm sunny day whilst I was a-choppin' wood, brother Joe come along wantin' to help, and I told him he dast not put his foot on the block. But he did it and I swung the axe, sliced his boot, and nearly chopped his toe clean off.

Paw was floored and said I warn't too old fer a switchin' and went to fetch a hickory, but I jes walked off and clum up to the Nettle Knob to do some thinkin'. Nothin' was a-goin' right, and I reckon I reached the end of it.

Afore I got to the top I set awhile nigh a little run. It was jes a trickle but was commencing its way to the river and the ocean, and it put me in mind of how religion must have changed over all the ages. Started out all clear and simple, like the water up there on the banch a the mountain, not deep and wide and cloudy, like church learnin' has got, so a body cain't figure the half a it.

I always believed there was a God, and I prayed every now and then, but mostly they was jes words. That day I meant it when I asked God to help me, 'cause the tears came a-runnin' down as iffen they would never stop. I told Him I had to jes give it up, 'cause I warn't fit to think hardly.

I stayed up there till nightfall, but I didn't git no answer. I figured I might as well go home and own up.

The first thing I did was tell Joe and Paw I was ashamed, and the tears started agin, but I catched them that time.

Paw put his hand on m'shoulder and said he jes come back from Moretz' mill and a letter was there at the post office that had come fer me. He handed it over and I saw it was from Silas.

The letter said the captain told all the boys to write their friends back home and tell them that the army would not punish those who come in, 'cept to dock them eleven dollars a month whilst they stayed away, and that Governor Vance was preparin' a proclamation promising all who returned a pardon, but severe punishment if they refused. I read it aloud fer Paw and Maw.

The news was like a sign to me, and that same night I packed all my army necessaries and laid out my uniform.

Sixty-three, Followed General Lee

Moss Neck, Virginia
10 January 1863

Dear Maw and Paw,

I am writin' to tell you that I reached Virginia safe. Rode the train with some other boys a-headin' to the camp. We are set up in a woods that belongs to a man the name of Corbin. Here fer the winter I reckon.

I almost feel like a stranger 'cause many a the old boys has died or gone home wounded, and some a the new ones ain't from Watauga. Come from Alexander County. Even Captain Farthing is dead. That was a sad thing, too, as he died the very same day he wrote a letter to resign and go home 'cause he was so terrible sick. Carroll and Silas and George and a few other boys is still here. They admired to see me back and give me a little welcome party with the cookies you sent along.

I ain't hardly had time to write 'cause fer a while we was a-choppin' trees nearly every minute. I reckon there ain't nary a one left in the whole county! They call choppin' "police duty." Ain't that somethin'? The army gives ever'thing a fancy name thinkin' we will be so glad to do it.

We also was ordered to assist in corduroying the roads, but afore the logs could be laid the snow had to be removed. On account a the distance we warn't able to return to camp fer the nights, and it was so cold and weathery that my feet has taken to botherin' me some. Paw, do you remember that old pair a boots in the loft? If there is a way to send them to me, I would shore be pleased.

'Cept for that, I'm tolerable, but a heap a sickness is on us, it's fearful to wake at night and hear the men 'round me a-coughin' with half-choked throats and moanin' and groanin' with pain. But don't you fret none fer me, 'cause I aim to be tough as a piggin string, as Paw says.

Did you get a letter from Adam? Iffen you did, tell me how he is faring. I asked here and 'bout where Adam's Fifty-eighth Regiment might be now, and I learnt they was still in Tennessee, at Big Creek Gap fer the winter.

I will be lookin' fer some writin' from Isaac and Joe, and will close this now and subscribe.

Your faithful son,
Alf

* * *

We passed the winter at Moss Neck a-workin' on the roads or doin' picket duty nigh the Rappahannock River. Sometimes I read a little, played cards, or fixed m'pine-needle mattress. Me and George even made sport by racing lice on the flat side a his canteen. The worst thing in the world was tryin' to git shed a the fleas and graybacks. The joke told was we got vexed and commenced killin' them, but as a hundred of them bugs came to each one's funeral, we gave it up as a bad job.

One time I visited the sutler's tent to see the *Southern Illustrated News*, and I bought a fried pie that cost four times what it was worth. It was s'moldy that when I broke it open it looked like it was full a cobwebs, and the dadburn sutler wouldn't return my money.

Seems a queer thing a-lookin' back, but I recall when several of us went down to the river on a pretty Sunday and traded tobacco fer coffee with the enemy by sailin' toy boats acrost with the cargo.

Some a the memories are good ones, but I reckon that winter was when I started to degenerate, too. I never woulda thought a gambling back home, but at Moss Neck I learnt to love it, 'specially chuck-a-luck!

And I even liked to hear the dirty jokes ever'body told, tho' I never could remember enough to pass them on. When you don't have no women around, I guess that's what it always comes to.

The first thing I ever stole from a man was at Moss Neck. I had to get the practice in 'cause the men in the army was the most scientific stealers I ever did see. What I took was a likeness of a nude woman. Somebody later on stole it offen me, but whilst I had it I liked to cover the face and pretend it might be Hettie. Shameful things to be a-thinkin' on now! But that's the way it was.

Some a the cities turned evil, too. I recall readin' that the mayor of Richmond said never was a place so changed than the Capitol. "Go on to the Square any afternoon, and you may see these women promenading up and down the shady walks jostling respectable ladies into the gutters." All the sin sort of fascinated me then.

Mostly tho', I wrote letters when I had m'own time, jes to keep in touch with the world back home. But I shore wisht Paw or Maw knowed how to write so more letters woulda come to me. Paw said when he was a boy ever'body was too busy clearin' land fer schoolin'. I reckon I warn't as bad off as some boys who got no letters atall never.

At least m'mind was at ease after Hettie come to see how I jes had to go back to the regiment.

***

Moss Neck, Virginia
1 March 1863

Dear Hettie,

Your box come yesterday and I am proud to have the writin' paper you sent as there ain't nary a bit of it in this place. But I will have to hide it 'cause some boys here would steal a chew a tobacco outa your mouth iffen you opened it to yawn.

I got a letter from Isaac yesterday too, but it was a pitiful thing. Maw ain't heard nary 'nother word from Adam, and she frets over us somethin' awful. Says she is a-gonna' send a letter to General Lee to git us back home. And Isaac says he keeps devilin' her 'bout joinin' the Minute Men. Well, since this mean war is on us every man should be willin' to fight I reckon, but he hadn't orta join till he is older. It would break Maw's heart, and law, somebody has got to help on the place there.

A sight a fever is in all the camps and Carroll is down with it, too. Silas and me is doctorin' him and we don't reckon it's too bad.

Hettie, you fretted when I left wuther I would be true to you. Shoot! They ain't nary a girl 'round here noways, 'cept some a the officers' women.

Well, there is a few wild ones that follers the camps but I wouldn't touch one a them with a ten-foot pole. They is the ugliest, shaggy-headed, dirty wretches you ever seed.

I am the same as always, tho' I will admit I set into cussin' and drinkin' now and then, but that jes comes natural here. Mostly, all I think 'bout is you and good old Watauga.

I do love you so Hettie, and when I git home I want us to get married iffen you will have me. I calculate your Maw would be happy 'cause she likes me more than any boy you ever knowed.

Well, I must close now. I hope you can read this poor letter as I am seated on the ground and a-writin' on my knee.

Your affectionate friend,
Alf

Writin' on the envelope! Tell little Jake I thank him fer the fish hooks. Me and Silas went fishing and caught us a catfish and some eels.

* * *

I told a powerful lie in that letter!

I warn't at Moss Neck a week afore I had the roll with a hooker, Mary Russell. I wonder iffen that was her real name. She was kindly handsome with black eyes and hair, but she musta weighed more'n 180 pounds. She sashayed all 'bout in a plaid dress with her hoops and shakers on.

Warn't all my fault I reckon. We was all antic-like one night and a-talkin' bawdy, and the boys could tell I ain't had no woman yet, so they set the whole thing up.

They gathered some money together and paid the wench, then bantered me fer several days to go see her, but I paid it no mind.

Afore I knowed it, one night they jes hog-tied me and carried me to Mary's tent. "Russell's Bake Oven" we called it. They throwed me in like Daniel to the lions and took off.

She was far gone in drink and got right to it. "You here fer some horizontal refreshments?" she said with her eyes squinched up. "They tell me you ain't old enough, but 'the younger the back the stiffer the horn', I say." The Lord knowed I didn't aim to, but it happened.

Later on I hated that m'first time was with sech a trollop, and I fretted fer weeks that I might git the disease some several a the men got.

And wouldn't you know it, jes when I was feelin' the most guilty a letter come from Maw. Course Isaac or Joe did the writin' but the words was Maw's, and they ain't nothin' will make a man feel more shame than to think on your own Mother after you did somethin' wicked. I don't even recall the most of it, 'cept it was a long one. Said she and Paw prayed fer her boys every day, and how hurt she was 'cause they warn't no time fer the infare after Adam's weddin' afore he took off. "There is some epidemic in the camp where Adam is, near Jacksboro, Tennessee, this winter," she

39

wrote. "Adam ain't like you, Alf. When he was a jes a child he was always took down with somethin' or other, like m'baby Ransom who was only three years old when he went to heaven." She fretted if I was warm enough and promised to send me a tack quilt when she got it pieced, but I never did git it. Then she told: "Keith Blalock scoutin' with Yankees through the mountains was wounded by some men who followed him up to a rail pen under the Grandfather." He made his escape on up the mountain and figured my Uncle Robert was the one who shot him, and he swore revenge.

I was glad when a letter from Maw came, 'cause there warn't many, but I always felt sorta lonely when I finished it.

✳ ✳ ✳

Fredericksburg, Virginia
25 March 1863

Dear Hettie,

I jes learnt some bad news, the saddest that has come my road. Adam is dead. It was the measles I reckon 'cause he was on outpost in the Cumberland Mountains all through the winter and the exposure was terrible. And I am the one who told him it would be better to go with the army into the mountains!

He died in a hospital at Clinton, Tennessee, 5 March. They sent his clothes home, and $62 that he had in his pocket.

I remember way back when I first left home, the last thing he ever said to me. I was a-headin' out the door and he said, "Now Alf, you take care a yourself." That's the last word he ever told me.

Whatever you do fer your brother don't ever regret it 'cause he's the best friend you'll ever have. I don't care what kinda friends I have in this world, I'll never have one that will ever come up to my brother.

Alf

Jordan's bank stayed close to me then, fer cousin Carroll died the same month, on the last day it was.

They had put him in a hospital tent and Silas and me was at his side every chance we had, but he jes went down worse every single hour. We saw them carry two or three outa that death ward every day!

The doctor treated him with quinine and opium one time, and then liquor after that. Told us jes to help him rest easy and change the mustard plaster and keep his face dry. He was in a fever and a-shakin' with chills all at onest, and he kep' coughin' up a green and yeller spittle. It was powerful hard on Silas, and I ain't never forgot it neither.

Most a the time he was outa his head. I recall we even had to laugh onest when he babbled on 'bout Silas a-tryin' to git him to jump ten feet offen a haystack onto the back of a mean cow. Silas said it did happen, when he was 'bout seven year old.

The last time we saw him alive we was jes struck when he looked at both of us with clear eyes and said, "One down, two to go." He was gone the same day and was buried at the camp along with some other boys who died.

We followed the body to the grave with our guns reversed and fired off a salute, and then the chaplain spoke a few words, but you could tell he didn't know nothin' 'bout Carroll.

I wonder was that the way it was fer Adam?

Come spring, the enemy set up demonstrations at Fredericksburg, so we was ordered up and marched a few hours to the second line a works nigh there.

I could see the Yankees in the flat down below, near thirty thousand of them.

I think it was jes then I made up my mind to be the best damn soldier I could, fer Adam's honor.

Some a the enemy split off to the west to try and flank us, so we countered, marchin' 'bout ten miles toward Chancellorsville, what was no more'n a crossroads and a tavern.

* * *

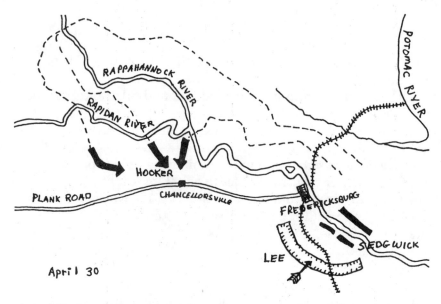

April 30

Joseph Hooker, who succeeded Burnside at the head of the Federal Army, left part of his force under Sedgwick as a decoy, and marched westward across the Rappahannock to outflank the Confederates. (➤➔ 37th Regiment)

Moss Neck, Virginia
10 May 1863

Dear Maw and Paw,

We was in the worst ever battle a this war a week ago.

On Friday mornin', 1 May, we marched in a heavy fog from Fredericksburg along the Plank Road to the front line near Chancellorsville, where the Yanks was fortified. We throwed skirmishers out and spent the night.

At first light on Saturday we rolled up our blankets, gulped cold rations, and waited! That was the usual way fer the army, hurry up and wait!

Then at 8 a.m. we started with General Stonewall Jackson on a flank move around the enemy. We went near eleven mile round the whole Yankee army in broad daylight, and we was strung out fer miles like sittin' ducks.

I was right fagged out cause we had only three short rests. That was the grandest move any army ever made!

Jes as we reached the turnpike in the rear a the Yanks,

the prettiest rainbow spread acrost the sky. Like a omen.

Then 'bout sunset, we made our battle lines. General Jackson stood directly at the head a our regiment and all our eyes was on him.

Then the enemy opened a mean artillery fire and we was ordered to lie down quick. The Yanks had over forty pieces a cannon to throw at us, and as our regiment was the lead one in Lane's Brigade, it was unmerciful on us.

Jes then John Mitchell, a man in our company from Alexander County, commenced prayin'. He went down low and loud, loud and strong. You ain't never heared sech a prayer come outa nobody as come outa that man.

Well, fortunate fer us, the cannon fire lasted but a short time and we took our place in the road ready to move. Then little George Patrick made a speech: "Gentlemen, I want to tell you all somethin' and I want these officers to remember it. I am never goin' to stay in another place such as that! You may shoot me iffen you want to, but if you take me in another place like that, I am a-gonna' leave!" Then he paused a bit and said, "But gentlemen, didn't Mitchell pray?" And he laughed as iffen they was no sech a thing as cannon balls!

The woods in front of us was large oaks and in the rear was a pine thicket, and to the left was thick scrubby brush. We moved down the road whilst our skirmishers in front kep' up a battle into the night. With all the confusion in the woods, our boys didn't know that General Jackson and some other officers had gone to the front. So in the firing in the dark he was shot by some of our own brigade, boys a the Eighteenth Regiment. They thought the General was the enemy 'cause a the direction he come from. We don't know yet how bad it is but we fear the worst, and the men a the Eighteenth feel terrible 'bout it. We spent the night crouched behind the works to rest and think on the next day.

Come mornin' we moved forward as if on parade and drove the enemy in front of us. In the rout I captured $5 worth a paper and envelopes.

After they was defeated at every point we returned to

43

camp at Moss Neck, where we found all our shelters broken down or took away by the enemy.

Our company lost twenty-six soldiers and we ain't got but fifty-five left. Silas was shot and kilt too.

I am thankful to be alive, and I hope to see all a you again.

Tell howdy to any one who asks 'bout me.

Your faithful son,
Alf

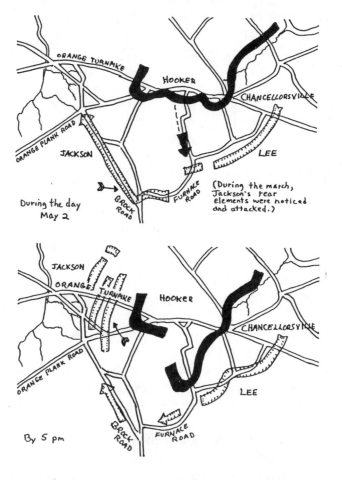

Jackson's flanking march of 2 May 1863

***

"Silas was kilt too." It's strange to read it thata way. So cold. One minute he was at m'side, on the left, and the next he was gone and I never seed him alive or dead agin. All the dead was buried on the field, but I warn't on the detail. I reckon I ain't thought on it much after that.

We stayed at Moss Neck fer 'bout a month where we learnt that General Jackson died from his wound.

One thing the battle proved was our General Lee was better'n anyone the Yankees had, and with half a the soldiers, too!

Well! Look here, a story somebody cut out of a newspaper and saved:

> Never have I seen men fight more gallantly, and bear fatigue and hardship more cheerfully. I shall always feel proud of the noble bearing of my brigade in the battle of Chancellorsville, the bloodiest in which it has ever taken part, when the Thirty-third discharged its duties so well as skirmishers, and when the Eighteenth and Twenty-eighth gallantly repulsed two night attacks made by a vastly superior number, and when the Seventh and Thirty-seventh vied with each other as to who should first drive the vandals from their works.
>
> — General James H. Lane

***

Moss Neck, Virginia
1 June 1863

Dear Hettie,

I don't know iffen you will believe this or not, but I been made a fifth sergeant and I am proud to death, 'cause even tho' I hate this war, I have determined to be the best soldier

45

there ever was. Fer m'brother and Silas and Carroll.

Tell your Maw and little Jake about the promotion. He will be happy as a dead pig in the sunshine, won't he?

We heared that General Jackson died two or three weeks ago, so General Lee has reorganized the army. Now we are in the Third Corps under General A. P. Hill.

This ain't much of a letter 'cause I am a-goin' on duty in a few minutes, but I wanted you to have the news.

Nobody can be as lonesome as me, and I want you to know that I could be satisfied to see you and hold your hand but one more time.

Your affectionate friend,
Alf

* * *

With all the fightin' in Virginia, the place was so torn down we could scarcely git no food. So, come June, General Lee turned us around and marched us into the Shenandoah Valley a-headin' north.

* * *

Fayetteville, Pennsylvania
29 June 1863

Dear Brother,

I hope this letter finds you well and a-workin' hard fer Paw.

You asked me 'bout the Minute Men. Well, only fifty-four of us is left now. We had a quiet spell at the camp as iffen they warn't no war a-goin' on atall. Even traded newspapers with the Yanks. And their band and ours played music time about acrost the river one evenin', songs fer both sides, and then they ended it together with "Home Sweet Home." It was sad. Both a the armies shouted and cheered at the end.

On 6 June we was back at the old line at Fredericksburg a-watchin' some a the Federals that had crost the Rappahannock to our side. After they recrost the river we went on a-marchin' north.

That was 15 June, and then we took off fer Pennsylvania. We moved so fast and the sun was a-scorchin' so much that we stirred up a tornado a dust. 'Twas so bad you couldn't touch your teeth together. Ever'one was a-crowdin' front and back. Some fell out and died right by the roadside.

We crost the Potomac River at Shepherdstown on 25 June and reached Fayetteville in two days, a-shoutin' and hurrahin' as usual. That's where we are now, jes settin' a bit. Seems like we had breakfast in Virginia, a bottle a whiskey in Maryland, and supper in Pennsylvania. I am all fagged out now fer certain.

There is plenty to eat here tho', 'cause we ain't left nary a hog, chicken, turkey, goose, duck, or onion behind. And I ain't never seed so much wheat a-growin'!

They say the Yankees has another new general. Name is Meade. I calculate he won't last a bit longer than the othern. This army a General Lee jes ain't a-gonna' be whupped and that is God's truth!

We heared there is a shoe factory over yon at a place called Gettysburg. Well, after all our marchin' we shore can use them shoes, so one a our divisions plans to go at sunup to git all they can tote. There is some several men got nary a thing on their feet 'cept red cracks in the heel. Isaac, I must stop now and git some rest. Write to me as soon as you git this.

> Your faithful brother,
> Alf

* * *

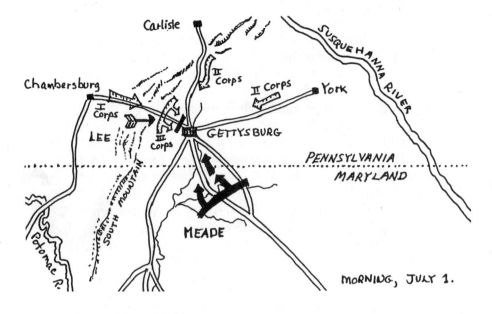

The vanguards of George Meade and Robert E. Lee's armies collided accidentally at the crossroads town of Gettysburg, 1 July 1863.

Gettysburg, Pennsylvania
4 July 1863

Dear Maw and Paw,

I don't know iffen I can git this letter done and sent off, but I am a-gonna' try.

Hell is not far from Gettysburg.

We came here Wednesday and found some of Heth's division busy with the enemy. Them boys had gone there a-lookin' fer a shoe factory. When we saw the fightin' we made a battle line behind them right quick and marched forward.

We moved toward a little rise called Seminary Ridge. The Yanks threw double canister charges at us, and it stopped us fer a minute, but we come on agin, yellin' like demons and even chargin' over the dead and wounded men. We finally took the ridge and that was all fer us on that day.

On Thursday the second we held our ground all day under heavy cannon fire, but we had no other fightin', tho' we could hear battles all around. And through it all we listened to the band a the Twenty-sixth playin' fer their regiment over yon—cannons and music together, it was odd.

Yesterday mornin' our brigade was sent to the right to assist General Longstreet. We made our lines at 9:00 a.m. Our major general was wounded the day afore, so another general, name of Trimble, was sent to command us. He rode down the line and made little speeches, sayin' tho' he was a stranger to us, he would lead us up on Cemetery Hill, where the Yanks was, at three o'clock.

'Bout eleven o'clock it had come a quiet and stillness as if 'twas the Sabbath day. It was only broke by a little cannon fire in front a us. Fightin' over some barn.

Then at one o'clock the loud boom of two cannons was heard away off to the right. They was our signal guns.

Then commenced our whole artillery to a-firin'. We had more than 150 cannon a-blastin' at the Yankees. You ain't never heared sech a racket in all the days a your life. It scared a body to death to hear it. The whole earth was a-shakin' like it was the end a time. The Yanks was firin', too, so the captain hollered, "Stay down!" Lord, I knowed to do it! After two long hours a that the firin' stopped jes as quick as it started. That is when we moved forward.

Oh, Paw, it was like we war a-goin' to hell or glory! It was a grand sight as far as the eye could see, two lines a soldiers with waving blue and red banners marchin' into the jaws a death. I was in the second line. It was smotherin' hot.

We came outa the woods under order not to holler the Rebel yell, so, silent like demon haints, towards the Emmitsburg Road we went.

All of a sudden fire was a-comin' aginst our flank! We all herded to the center but kep' our eyes set on the Yankee line straight ahead. The enemy fire was like a hail storm, and our line seemed to be meltin' away all the while. You could hear a moan from the whole field above the shootin'. But we marched as iffen we was on drill!

We passed over the remains a the line in front of us, then someone hollered, "Three cheers fer the Old North State," and we all sent up a shout.

The Yanks was waitin' jes over the road. We drove them from it and back to a fence, but their fire was right in our faces and we couldn't break their lines, Paw, and we tried and tried. Pretty soon we began to fall back from the fence when the order come to retreat.

So back down the slope we went. At every moment guns, swords, and human flesh was a-flyin' above the earth. But we marched back slow, in almost as good order as we came on.

Our brigade general, Lane, got a message from Trimble what said, "If hell can't be taken by the troops I had the honor to command today, it can't be done atall!"

We stopped at the top a Seminary Ridge and dug in to wait. Less than forty is left in our company, and lotsa other ones is worse off than that. But if the Yankees attack, we aim to fight to the last man!

Two or three hours ago it come a hard rain. Law, it jes poured. Maybe it will wash the blood from the grass.

Your faithful son,
Alf

Map Page 51: Battle of Gettysburg, Afternoon of 2 July 1863

While the Thirty-seventh Regiment held their position on Seminary Ridge, action was furious on other fronts. The Second Corps struck Meade's right on Culp's Hill while the First Crops assailed the left, driving the Federals from the wheat field and peach orchard. The whole left of Meade's battle line came unraveled, but quick action by the Federal Fifth Corps in taking control of the Round Tops thwarted the Confederate attack by the narrowest of margins. In the end, Culp's Hill and the Round Tops were held, and a thrust at Cemetery Ridge by part of A.P. Hill's Third Corps was beaten back by Meade's forces.

Map Page 52: The Battle of Gettysburg, Afternoon of 3 July 1863

The climax of the battle came when some fifteen thousand men under general control of George Pickett struck the Federal position on Cemetery Ridge after 140 Confederate guns carried on an intensive bombardment. Aiming to strike the center of Meade's line, the Confederates hit a position too strong to be carried with the numbers available, and their costly repulse ended the battle.

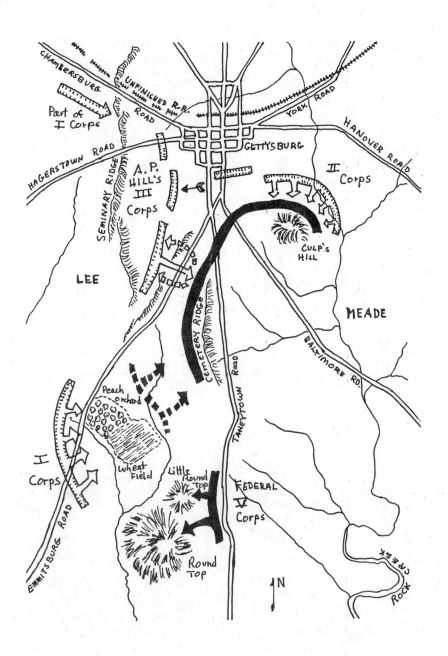

CHAMBERSBURG

UNFINISHED R.R. ROAD

YORK ROAD

HANOVER ROAD

Part of I Corps

HAGERSTOWN ROAD

SEMINARY RIDGE

A.P. HILL'S III Corps

GETTYSBURG

II Corps

CULP'S HILL

LEE

CEMETERY RIDGE

MEADE

BALTIMORE RD.

TANEYTOWN ROAD

Peach Orchard

I Corps

Wheat Field

Little Round Top

FEDERAL V Corps

EMMITSBURG ROAD

Round Top

N

ROCK CREEK

51

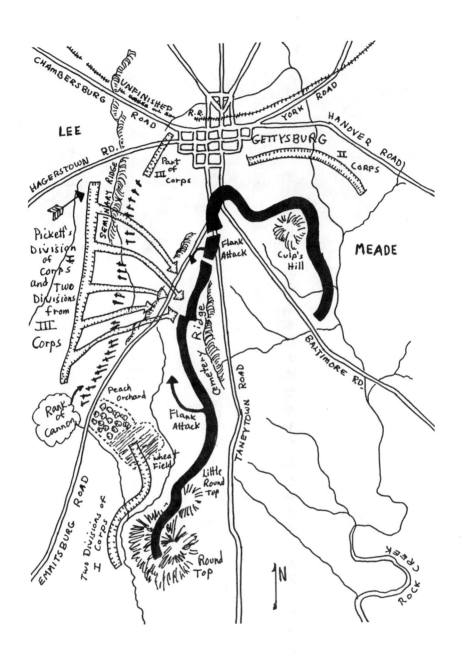

CHAMBERSBURG ROAD

UNFINISHED ROAD

R.R.

LEE

HAGERSTOWN RD.

SEMINARY RIDGE

Part of III Corps

GETTYSBURG

YORK ROAD

HANOVER ROAD

II CORPS

MEADE

Pickett's Division of I Corps and Two Divisions from III Corps

Flank Attack

Culp's Hill

Cemetery Ridge

BALTIMORE RD.

Rank of Cannon

Peach Orchard

Flank Attack

Wheat Field

TANEYTOWN ROAD

EMMITSBURG ROAD

Two Divisions of I Corps

Little Round Top

Round Top

N

ROCK CREEK

Whilst the battle at Gettysburg went on, we had barely a thing to eat, so on the night a the third we crawled out on the field after dark where the dead and wounded lay, and took the haversacks offen those who was kilt in the fight that day. They was nearly all full a hoe-cakes. Some that we found was stained with blood where it had run into the sacks from their wounds. But we was so hungry we didn't stop fer that.

* * *

Orange Court House
21 July 1863

Dear Maw and Paw,

When we left Pennsylvania we slogged all night under a drenchin' rain. It was a long, long sad gray march through the South Mountain passes. The next day General Lee hisself rode jes in front a our regiment the whole time. I kep' a-watchin' him. I figure he is proud of us anyway.

I heared we lost more than a third a the army at Gettysburg, but we ain't got outa heart disregardless. When we come to rest at Hagerstown we was plumb beat out, but we still hoped to git up another fight. We want our revenge.

Whilst we was a-settin' there, a man, name is Tom Norwood from Company A, come into camp. He was shot through the breast and captured, but here he comes, a-marchin' in, disguised in the most silly suit a clothes you ever seed. He was bad hurt with his wound, but he had snuck off and hoofed straight through the enemy lines some way or 'nother. We was so proud to see him we all cheered and petted over our Tom. Then he was invited to headquarters where he took a cup a coffee with General Lee.

We made breastworks the best we could in the rain, and had some skirmishin' whilst a-waitin' fer the Potomac waters to go down. On Monday it was some better, so we pulled outa the trenches and fixed us a bridge.

You orta seed what we throwed acrost that river! We used scraps and all sech as this and that to build it. Then it come to rain some more and we was in a main misery. Had to keep our hands on the back a the man ahead jes to know when to move and when to halt! At every step I went nearly up to my knees in mud. Finally we got acrost the bridge, and then we cut the thing loose.

Right now we are in camp nigh Orange Court House a-lickin' our wounds and doin' picket duty at Mortin's Ford. A lotsa men is hurt bad or sick, and some has been skulkin' off to go home. Jes yesterday five from our company deserted. They say they is a-gonna' help with the crops and then come back. Well, some do, and some don't. I cain't help but think on it too. I would a heap ruther be there as here, but I ain't a-gonna' be no deserter.

Now here's some good news. George Patrick was promoted to corporal on account a his good conduct. George will have his fun, but he is a good soldier too. And can you guess? I been promoted too, one notch higher, to fourth sergeant.

They ain't been as much carousin' and drinkin' lately. I figure it's 'cause we are all thinkin' more on the Lord than we ever did afore. Services and hymn-singin' is held nearly every night now, and many a the boys join in.

Well, I will close now as I am nearly off the paper. I miss you all dearly.

Your faithful son,
Alf

* * *

Come fall we was right pert agin, so General A. P. Hill put on a Grand Review of the Third Corps fer General Lee. Word of it spread through all the towns around and thousands a civilians and soldiers gathered on the plain at Orange Court House to watch it. Seventeen regimental bands played. 'Twas on a Friday in September, and I jes filled with pride when the Thirty-seventh took its turn to break and parade afore the review stand.

Nobody watchin' or marchin' on that day doubted that the Army of Northern Virginia could beat Meade's Army of the Potomac.

We spent the rest a the year movin' here and there in Virginia. In October we made a fake towards Washington that caused the Yanks to build defenses. Later we formed a battle line at Bristoe Station, but was not in the bloody fight that took place.

On our return to the Rappahannock our regiment was detailed to destroy the Orange and Alexandria Railroad. We ripped up the rails and stacked the ties and set them afire. Then we laid the rails on till the iron glowed red hot. Half a dozen of us grabbed each end and ran to a telegraph pole or tree and ran surround it, bendin' the rail three or four times. It was hard work but kindly fun too.

We went into winter quarters at Liberty Mills on the Rapidan River, in Doc Newman's woods, and there I was promoted agin, to third sergeant!

We had no peace fer awhile 'cause Meade crost the river and forced us to march to Mine Run and fortify strong acrost his front. That was in November, and we stayed several days in a constant blizzard.

My boots had give out and I had to wrap m'feet in rags. I never suffered so much from the cold as that time, but finally Meade recrost the river and we returned to camp fer the winter.

Sixty-four, Had Enough of War

I Clipped this from a newspaper:

Resolutions of the 37th North Carolina Regiment

37th Regiment N.C. Troops,
10 February 1864

At a meeting of the 37th Regiment of North Carolina Troops, held this day, the following committee having been appointed to propose resolutions for the consideration of the meeting:

Captain Wm. T. Nicholson, Company E; Captain D. L. Hudson, Company G; Captain A. J. Critcher, Company B; Sergeant J. M. Black, Company A; Private Rufus Holdaway, Company A; Sergeant H. D. Hagaman, Company B; Private P. W. Turnmine, Company B; Sergeant J.W. Alexander, Company C; Private J.W. Barnett, Company C; Private K.M. Hasty, Company D; Private K.M. Dees, Company D; **Sergeant Alford Green, Company E;** Private James C. Coffey, Company E; Sergeant R.

M. Staley, Company F; Corporal J. C. Duncan, Company F; Corporal C. C. Pool, Company G; Private A. Campbell, Company G; Sergeant J. J. Ormand, Company H; Sergeant R. B. Tucker, Company H; Sergeant J. C. Flow, Company I; Private D. L. McCord, Company I; Private D. H. Douglas, Company K; Private S. V. Box, Company K.

Captain W.T. Nicholson, chairman of the committee, reported the following resolutions as recommended by all of the committee, except Sergeant J.W. Alexander, of Company C. He recommends none in lieu of them:

Resolved, That we are still determined that our country shall be a free and independent nation, notwithstanding the absurd proclamations of Abraham Lincoln; and we do hereby pledge anew our property, our lives, and our honor and our all, never to submit to Abolition tyranny nor Yankee rule.

Resolved, That we originally enlisted as a regiment for twelve months because we believed that our country needed us in the field, and that we afterwards re-enlisted for two additional years of the war before the Conscript Bill had been introduced in Congress, because we thought she still needed us; and that now, actuated by the same belief, we tender to the Government of our country our services in the field for the war unconditionally and without reserve.

Resolved, That we are perfectly satisfied with the present organization of our army, and have unlimited confidence in the skill, bravery and patriotism of our Generals.

Resolved, That while we endeavor to do our duty, we shall expect the authorities to do theirs; we shall expect them to see all deserters and skulkers from our ranks shot at the stake in disgrace. We shall expect them to allow us to visit our homes once every twelve months, at such times as the exigencies of the service will permit; and shall expect them to feed, clothe, and shoe us, and not to allow worthless subordinates to make us suffer by their indolence.

Resolved, That we are ready to endure without a murmur all necessary hardships and privations which the good of the cause may demand.

Resolved, That we call confidently upon all good people at home to give us their sympathy and support, to send us food to sustain life and recruits to fill our wasted ranks.

Resolved, That a copy of these resolutions be sent to the Congress of the Confederate States, to the Secretary of War, through regular official channels, to His Excellency Governor Vance of North Carolina, and to the newspapers for publication.

The above resolutions were then submitted to the regiment and opportunity was allowed for a fair and free expression of opinion, when it was found that out of nearly 500 who were present, only about twenty were opposed to the resolutions.

The resolutions were accordingly declared adopted, and the meeting adjourned.

Wm. M. Barbour,
Colonel 37th N. C. T.,
President of Meeting

* * *

Liberty Mills, Virginia
20 March 1864

Dear Isaac,

I was proud to git your letter and I am glad you are all well. Today is Sunday and I am a-restin' in the peace and quiet.

I was promoted agin, to second sergeant, and now it's jes one more step up, and that is to orderly sergeant.

Shoot! Iffen I am in this army a week or two longer I will make a general!

Durin' the winter there was a deep snow and the enemy kep' quiet, so it's been peaceful.

A few men has enlisted and a few returned till I reckon 'bout sixty is in the company now. It is still a hard time here as there is sech a little bit a food to eat. The cook even found some shanks and necks in the beef so he was frettin' that soon they will commence to throwin' in the hoofs and horns. George says the meat proves so tough they orta issue files to us so we can hone our teeth fer better chewin'.

Now I will tell you 'bout our snowball battle. It was as wild as it could be and we laughed till our sides plumb ached!

Regiments was formed and the officers wore their side arms. The Thirty-third marched from their camp to that a the Seventh and captured it without a fight, and the two a them demanded the surrender of the Eighteenth, which was given right off. They then sent a challenge to the Twenty-eighth and Thirty-seventh. We accepted right quick and gave a loud cheer, then formed a line of battle on the edge of a hill in front a the camp and waited. The snow was shoe mouth deep and made the best snow balls.

The three assaulting regiments soon appeared acrost the field and attacked. But one smack-dab volley from us drove them back down the hill. They returned two or three times till finally our center broke, and they drove us back to a creek and through it.

We tried to check them there, but they come right acrost and drove us back to our quarters. Then the battle commenced in earnest!

We pulled out the daubing from our shacks, picked up rocks, fought with sticks and anything we could git, but it was no go. They drove us outa our camps and plundered them in regular Yankee style. General Lane, seein' the fight was gettin' serious, ordered the battle to cease.

60

I reckon we have some good times here at old Liberty Mills.

Isaac, I must close now. Write agin.

Your faithful brother,
Alf

P.S. Ever'body is growin' a moustache and a beard, so I am tryin' to raise one too. It's a sorry thing so far, but we will see.

✳ ✳ ✳

That was in '64? The same spring President Grant was give command a the Federal armies.

✳ ✳ ✳

Wilderness, Virginia
8 May 1864

Dear Maw and Paw,

I reckon all good times come to a end, and ours ended four days ago a Wednesday mornin', 4 May.

Even afore our bread was baked, bugles and drums called us to fall in, and we set out east along the Orange Plank Road toward Chancellorsville. It was a pretty day fer marchin', and come sunset we bivouacked fer the night at Verdierville.

"Bout noon on the fifth we heared heavy cannon, so we marched in columns and come upon dead Yankees by the roadside here and there. As we entered a thick woods nigh a little post town called Wilderness, there come a heavy firin' ahead of us. Our sharpshooters went in advance, swept through the wilds 'bout two hundred yards, and captured near 150 Yanks.

We was then withdrawn to the Plank Road to assist Heth's division which was bein' hit hard by overwhelming numbers. But we was the rear regiment, so we was kep' back by the road and had no part in the fight that afternoon.

Instead, we lay still and watched and listened to the heaviest musket shootin' I ever heared. Then the whole woods caught afire and commenced to roar like a cane-brake! You never seed nothin' to beat it, and they was fightin' in there too!

Come nightfall none a the brigades was in line, and some regiments was entirely lost. No one could tell one from the other. We don't know why nobody wouldn't order us to regroup or fix the lines. And we was so close to the enemy we could almost hear them breathing.

It was in this mixed-up mess that we took a heavy attack on the mornin' of the sixth. We was willin' to fight but we had no chance. 'Twas a muddle ever'where. Finally, our own troops pushed us back and we never did fire no gun!

Then about a hundred yards back here come Long-street's men and General Lee too! As they passed on through they throwed off on us somethin' awful. Said, "Do you boys belong to General Lee's army?" They wheeled into battle and drove the Yanks back into the wilderness.

We then found our brigade and fortified on the left a the Plank Road where we are now. Orders has come to move out so I close.

Alf

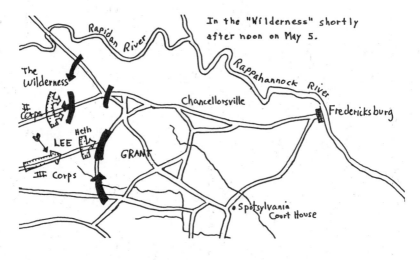

In the "Wilderness" shortly after noon on May 5.

Spotsylvania Courthouse, Virginia
15 May 1864

Dear Hettie,

It has poured rain every day fer five days and I am plumb miserable. It's a wonder I ain't dead and buried. The Lord has been good to me but I don't know why.

We left the wilderness battlefield 8 May in the afternoon 'cause the Yanks was tryin' to turn our right. We raced them to Spotsylvania and got here by noon Monday. We commenced cuttin' trees and throwin' up works nigh the courthouse.

At Thursday daylight, the twelfth, the enemy put up a heavy attack and broke one of our divisions, Johnson's. They captured most a them and then swept with a fury up the line towards our brigade.

The general shouted, "Hold your ground, the honor and safety of the army demands it!" With cheers and death-dealing aim we fired at them from the oblique whilst the rest a the brigade was a-firin' direct, till finally we stopped them and drove them from the field.

General Lane says we saved the whole battle jes then! We chased the Yanks three or four hundred yards beyond our works and into a piney brush, but then we was ordered to fall back. General Lee sat upon his horse jes in front of us.

A little later we was ordered back over the works agin towards a oak woods. As we advanced a shell exploded in Company D, killing the captain and eight men all at onest. General Lee was riding so close to us at the time we feared he would be kilt too.

We war movin' through the woods when a battery planted no more than a hundred yards off opened on us with grapeshot and canister. Then a officer from Company B rushed 'bout twenty yards in front with his hat in one hand and his sword in the other, a-shoutin' "Come on!" Some other officers then ran ahead with him and they led our regiment to the battery. We poured in one volley and kilt every man in there. It was the onliest time I ever seed officers lead a charge! They always stay in the rear to keep from bein' shot by their own men.

The enemy artillery fought bravely I will say, 'cause some was shot down whilst loadin' their cannon even as we stormed in. Four Napoleons and two rifles was in the battery, but we was unable to haul them off 'cause they warn't no road and no horses.

So, we wheeled to the left and surprised some Yanks who had jes charged our own works. Hettie, then and there in those oak woods come a battle with clubbed musket and bayonet, man to man, that there jes ain't no words to describe. There was blood splatterin' on ever'thing and ever'body. Godamighty!

And the mud was half up to my knees, so that by moving and thrashin' about, a wounded man was almost buried alive at my feet. Ever'one was a-tryin' to fight his way back to our works.

This bloody mess went on and on in the rain and smoke till past midnight when we finally got back. I ain't never gonna forget it.

When we charged that battery, our regiment captured two stands of colors. One was the Seventeenth Michigan, and the other one the Fifty-first Pennsylvania. That one was took by Lt. Wiggins of our company. He was captured by the Yankees but he made a escape and brought off the flag and some prisoners too! Law!

General Lane says he ain't never seed a regiment advance more beautifully than ours did in the face a such a murderous fire.

The rain is settin' in agin so I must close or this letter will get wet fer shore. I am a-thinkin' of you every day and hope I live to see you agin. But I am afeared there may be no more glory fer me 'cause the Minute Men and the whole army is a-dwindlin' fast. And the fire inside us is goin' too.

Your affectionate friend,
Alf

✳ ✳ ✳

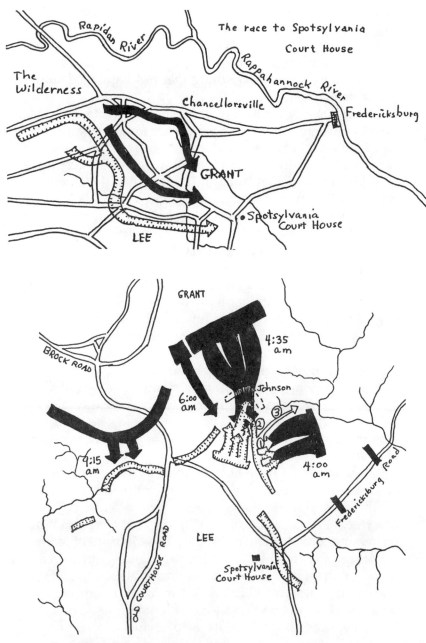

Spotsylvania Court House, 12 May 1864

(1) Repulsing early morning attack
(2) Counterattack on Federals who broke Johnson's line
(3) Fighting in the oak woods and capture of Federal battery

Petersburg, Virginia
24 June 1864

Dear Maw and Paw,

I want to tell you ever'thing that has happened since I wrote you last.

After dark on 21 May we marched from Spotsylvania Court House to Jericho Ford where we fought a battle. Our regiment was broke and run back twice by the enemy as we tried to advance through some woods. The rest a the brigade jes hung on but that's all. We did succeed in bringin' off all our dead and wounded.

Then we withdrew to Anderson's Station and set to work diggin' trenches, dug them directly through some right nice gardens, and we had some heavy skirmishin' fer a few days.

On Thursday, 2 June, we marched toward Cold Harbor and arrived in the afternoon jes in time to chase some Yankees off a little ridge called Turkey Hill. Then we dug in agin. We was parched and half starvin' by the time we finished. Our general, James Lane, was wounded by a sharpshooter that day and sent to a hospital.

Come Friday, the third, the enemy attacked at Cold Harbor but we was not in the fightin' 'cause of a thick swamp that kep' them out. But ever'where else the Yanks was mowed down line after line. They finally retreated about noon.

Dear folkses, I have become a hard man. Here the top of a man's skull a-hangin' by the hair from a limb ten feet off the ground, and yonder another man a-settin' behind a oak tree, his head shot off. And many that ain't dead, but jes wounded bad, the sun broiling down on them as they lay fer days with no help. I recall seein' one a our own soldiers leanin' aginst a fence. A shell had struck him and tore the whole stomach lining away, leavin' exposed his heart which was in motion. He seemed alive but he warn't. The new boys was all sickened at seein' it and vomited on the ground, but hell, sech sights as that do not affect me as they onest did. It sounds bad, but now I look on the carcass

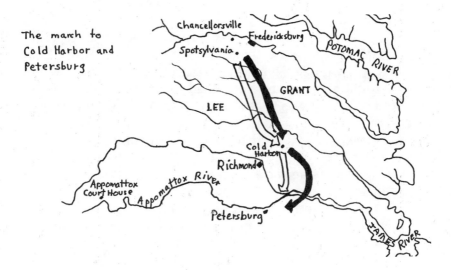

Above: 2 June 1864 March to Cold Harbor & 3 June 1864 Battle of Cold Harbor
Troops remained in defensive positions unitl 13 une when they began their
march to Petersburg.

Below: Took up position near Globe Tavern 18 June 1864

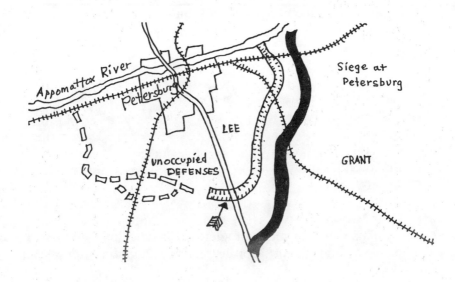

of a man with 'bout the same feelin' as I would have if it was a horse or a hog.

Come Monday, 13 June, General Lee ordered us to Petersburg where we arrived on the eighteenth near Globe Tavern. Law, this is a sorrowful place, too.

Right now we are entrenched 'bout the city a-tryin' to hold off the Yankees. Paw, it don't look so good to me no more.

I need not tell you that I dodge pretty often, fer you can see that very plainly by the blots in this letter. Jes count each blot a dodge and add in a few, fer I don't dodge every shot.

Yesterday we whupped some Yanks who was a-tryin' to git hold a the Petersburg and Weldon Railroad. They is lotsa skirmishin' here and I am tired and sick to death. And there ain't but a smidgen a food. A handful of black beans, a piece a sorghum, and half a dozen roasted acorns might be all I eat of a day. I recollect when we first come to the service we grumbled at fare we would now think was the greatest luxury.

If a body had told me afore this war that men could have borne fer month after month what we have, I would have thought him tetched.

Paw, I come into this war a boy, but God knows, I will come home a man iffen I can git there.

> Your faithful son,
> Alf

* * *

General Hospital No. 24
Richmond, Virginia
29 July, 1864

Dear Maw and Paw,

This won't be much of a letter. It's hard for me to use a pencil as I been shot. A bullet tore my shoulder outa place, the right arm. It happened yesterday nigh Gravel Hill, north a the James River, where we was sent to relieve some troops.

I was sent to Richmond, to Moore Hospital, where I am under a doctor, 'cept I ain't seed much a him. Too busy I reckon.

I got a misery every minute a the day and night, but no fever, and thank God, they don't have to cut my arm off like they do most a the time. Where I am right now I can look out the window and see the pile of arms and legs. Damn this war to hell!

Doc Graham of our regiment said I will probably be a-goin' home on furlough, but I jes don't hardly know when yet nor how I will git there.

Iffen you can, tell Hettie the news.

Your faithful son,
Alf

I come home safe, but with a powerful hurt in m'arm and dirty as a hog. Ever'body jes muched over me. I ain't never seed nobody s'good to me in my whole life, and I mended slowly. After a couple a weeks I was commonly well agin, tho' I have always kep' a bit a the rheumatiz in that shoulder, up to this day.

By September I could help Paw in the field with one arm and a half. It was 'bout then that cousin Leander heared I was home and come to see how I was faring.

He told me how the people was harassed beyond belief by Yankee lovers and deserters hidin' out and needing to be fed. And they was bold as hell 'cause they figured the war had swung to the side a the North. Then he commenced to tell 'bout his paw, Uncle Robert, and Blalock.

"Keith Blalock is a recruit officer now, fer some Michigan regiment over in Tennessee, and passing back and forth with his gang a skulkers. He had it in fer m'paw, and one day, was a while back, they met up on the road. Paw was a-drivin' his wagon from the Globe where we live now up to the other place, when Blalock shot him and broke his thigh. They left him fer dead but Paw managed to regain the wagon and turn it around somehow and git home.

They is nothin' but bad blood betwixt us and Blalock now. That damn home Yankee had a fight with Jesse Moore too, in Carroll Moore's orchard. Paw, you know, has married agin, to Julia Moore. Well, Jesse was wounded in the heel but Keith got his due, as his eye was shot out. But he's still scoutin'!

"The whole county has gone up, Alf. It's guerilla warfare."

Then Lee told me that he joined the Home Guard and how they was s'posed to guard the highways and river crossings and hunt out deserters wherever they could be reached, by orders from the Governor hisself.

Finally he come to the point. "Alf, I come to see iffen you might join with us seein' you are wounded and discharged, as we need all the help we can muster."

I showed him my paper, "It ain't a discharge, Lee, jes a furlough." I had no wish to join the Guard, but I kep' that to m'self.

"The eighth of September has come and gone, Alf," he said, learnin' what I already knowed. "Well, I ain't a-gonna say nor do nothin', but I can tell you they is many in the guard, and others too, that will not rest with you here free and easy. Did you know that Reubin Coffey has moved over here to Meat Camp? Said he was tired a the turmoil with his neighbors, but he is still a patriot. I'm jes warnin' you, that's all."

With that, he kinda hurried to make his leave. As if he didn't want to be seed visitin' with me no longer. Well, no matter. I had set my head never to go back to that son of a bitch war even afore I got home.

Things come together odd at times, 'cause it warn't long atall till I seed the very devil Lee spoke of. I was out huntin' game in a field nigh the Jefferson Road, and keepin' my eye out fer trouble, when along come a white horse with a girl ridin' it. She was 'bout my own age so I sidled over to take a gander, when who come directly up behind but Reubin Coffey! The girl was his daughter Millie.

This time, however, I had a gun, too. So we kinda stared in a standoff way fer a minute and then he left.

But I knowed that warn't the end of it, 'cause afore long visitors commenced arriving at our place, maybe twice a week or more. I was smart enough not to be there when they called. (We had set the children on the watch ever'day, and Maw fixed a signal, too.) When

70

there was still danger, the Lily quilt would hang on the shrub or the tree, and when it was safe she called the hogs.

I hated to see Maw and Paw pestered continuous thataway, tho', and there was no letup in sight. It's a terrible feelin' knowing you ain't safe in your own home.

Isaac was with me mosta the time then 'cause he was eighteen and they was after him too. He warn't in love with the war no more neither. He shore growed up in a hurry whilst I was gone. And good-lookin', too. We made us a reg'lar cave under a cliff up on Rich Mountain, and built a little fireplace in it and all. Isaac felled a tree acrost the entry and we covered it all over with branches. Iffen the farm was bein' watched, Maw would send Joe and Allen to us with food.

I only saw Hettie a few times 'cause I was afeared to bring trouble to her family, but we did spend half a the day together fer Christmas, or the day afore that, I don't recall which. 'Twas at her place and Jake kep' a watch out.

Seems as if all the talk over there was 'bout the war times too. You couldn't git away from it. Hettie went on a-tellin' me all 'bout somebody from Cove Creek s'posed to be kin a mine a way back. His granddad was a Green, she said. Some days I think I must be kin to ever'body surround here. So Hettie told it and I listened.

"Maw says he is some cousin of yours, Isaac Wilson, and they call him 'little Ike'. He was ploughin' in his field at the head a the north fork a Cove Creek, was early on this year, when some bush-whackers, Potter, Stout, and Guy boys I heared, slipped up and shot him dead. I recollect the Stout boys was Abraham, David, and Daniel. Good biblical names, too.

"Soon one a the Guy boys, Canada, was catched and hanged, along with some innocent friend a his. Then a little afterwards, old man Tom Stout, father of them boys was captured by the Home Guards and taken to Hiram Wilson's place over yon by Cove Creek, where he was kept. The next day some men, it was said who but I forget the names, was to take Stout to Camp Vance below Morganton, but they war told to take him 'the nigh way' and he warn't never seed agin."

Hettie's maw then chimed in with more a the same, so after awhile I jes went back up into the woods to clear m'head of it

71

all. But they had stuck it in m'mind and there it stayed, so I kep' a thinkin' on the fate of Tom Stout.

Afore sunset Isaac and me reached the edge a the new ground above the orchard and saw the quilt was gone. We was hungry as bears and raced each other, like we used to, acrost the frosted ground to the house. Ever'body had finished their vittles but Maw fixed us up the best she could. There ain't nothin' sweeter than a mother's smile.

We all made small talk fer awhile and I was glad of it. I promised Paw to rive some oak shakes and repair the roof come mornin', then me and Isaac went to sleep in our own bed.

I was at the barn afore daylight. I knelt down to see better the pieces of oak I was sortin', when I felt a stir behind me. Turnin' quick, I looked direct at a pair a army boots! I grabbed the hog rifle and took aim at a big round red face a-grinnin' back at me.

"George Patrick" I couldn't believe it . "You aimin' to git your head blowed off?" He jes laughed as always and we pumped hands like lost brothers.

"I never spected to see you alive agin. What brings you here?"

"I left, Alf. Couldn't take it no more. And Celie needs me. Here, take a look at this." I opened a paper and read it.

> My dear George. I have always been proud of you and since you joined the army I have been prouder of you than ever before. I would not have you do anything wrong for the world, but before God, George, unless you come home we must die. Last night I was awoked by Little George's crying. I called and said, what is the matter George? And he said O, Mamma, I am so hungry. I am getting thinner and thinner every day and before God, George, unless you come home, we must die.

I handed it back to him thinking a what I could say, but he went on, "I have to move at night and stay offen the main roads. I come this way to see wuther I might rest the day here in your barn."

"You're shorely welcome, George," I said, "come on to the house and set a spell."

Paw and ever'body knowed George right off on account a my letters, and Maw fixed him some scrapple. They asked him how the war was a-doin' and it didn't take no coaxin' fer him to answer.

"The sick languish alone in their tents, liable at any time to a drenchin' from the rain. Most ever'body has bare and bleeding feet. These boots I took offen a dead man. We was often without rations fer three or four days, and then rushed off on some wild goose chase, gen'rally in the night with our legs stiff as iron.

"Our spirit is broke now. Starvation, rags, dirt, and vermin can be borne fer a time, but when a man gits used to it, he is no longer a man but a animal."

We gave George the wash tub and then he settled in fer some sleep, as he was near delirious from havin' to force hisself to stay awake.

Later on when he was rested, Isaac and me had a heart-to-heart with him. I told him we was a-thinkin' on how we could go off someplace fer awhile. There was sech a scarcity a food fer all the children. Sometimes, when Maw went pokin' fer Irish taters or somethin' in the cellar out by the spring, and she thought nobody was lookin', her eyes liked to spilled over 'cause there was nothin' in there but a few bad roots.

"George, we ain't givin' a thing here 'cept a heap of disrepute to Paw, owin' to the Home Guard boys, who keep comin' bout like we was common bushwhackers. I reckon what decided it fer us was last week, when three a Major Bingham's home militia caught me and Isaac by surprise.

"We had jes come down to the house in the mornin', all frigid from the night, when up the lane come them fellers. We turned tail as quick as cats, but they spotted us and hollered fer us to halt, and opened fire. Now, jes then Sallie come outa the door to see what was the fuss, and one a their horses was s'close to the house, it knocked her clear offen the gallery, and out cold. She broke a tooth outa her head in the fall, and not one of them stopped to see if she was alive or dead.

"So we propose to shift somewheres else fer awhile, maybe Yancey or even Madison County, 'cause we heared round 'bout that the passes in them parts warn't guarded, and they ain't as many folkses that will bother you."

"Well," said George, stoppin' to think, "there is a way I might help you, and I wouldn't mind a bit a-goin' along, but only after I see to Celie and little George. When I can be certain they is cared fer, I will go with you, part way anyhow." We both spoke up and said we'd admire to have him join us, so he told us the plan.

"Now, I picked up some news whilst I was in Wilkesboro, from a old friend, 'bout this gang a horse thieves that carry their trade from Taylorsville to Cincinnati, in Ohio. And Boone is one a their headquarters. They will be a-stoppin' over there come Thursday, I was told. I reckon Celie has waited this long fer me, she can wait that little more iffen you want me to help."

We spent the next night plannin' our course. Paw and Maw was not happy atall 'cause a the risk, but they saw it was jes as bad with our hidin' out on the mountain. Me and Isaac had set our minds, and George mapped it out.

Afore the time was up, I had to see Hettie onest more, so I sneaked over the first chance that come along. Her Maw was good to us and give us some privacy.

Hettie bawled when I told of our plans and begged to go with me, but there was no way a that. All I could do was try and soothe her, but she would have none of it.

We finally jes let it go, and laid close together awhile by the fire. She was full a warmth, and comfort, like I never dreamt of. "Hettie," I found the words, "it's a bad time, I know, but I do want you so." She run her fingers up and down my back, and explored some, and with nary a word, told me to have her.

She cried agin when her Maw and Jake come home, and I left.

Sixty-five, Lucky to Be Alive

Fortunate fer us the clouds was heavy and the night jes black as we crept down amongst the rocks from Howard's Knob to Boone. Some old unfinished house built by Will Fletcher a while back was the hiding place fer the gang.

We had no trouble findin' it, but we had to be careful. Didn't know how many men was there. 'Twas the dead a night with no noise 'cept a hoot owl off somewheres, and we fretted over every stick that snapped under our feet.

We split up with George goin' around the house and me the nigh side, while Isaac backed us. George had his side arm and we toted rifles. We could barely make out that there was two a them in there, a-sleepin' like babies. A closer look showed several empty bottles a whiskey and we knowed we was in luck.

The whole thing was too easy. We jes picked us up a plank and struck them over the head and called Isaac in. After hog-tieing them up we helped ourselves to their saddles and three stout-lookin' horses.

George relieved them a their side arms and give them to me. I kep' the Colt pistol and handed Isaac the Spiller-Burr.

That night we took the public road outa Boone to the west till we come to Ward's Holler, then we turned up and followed the

Watauga River a ways. It was the middle a the night, and George thought it best not to try to git all the way to his place fer it would put a scare into Celie. So we bedded down in a little pine grove on Long Ridge to wait till near mornin', and to git some shut-eye iffen we could.

I was so tired that I dozed under in a minute, but then, all a sudden, Isaac shooked me awake. "Listen," he said. There was some talkin' and laughter a-comin' down the path. Sounded like a whole company. I looked around. "Where's George?"

"He took the horses off a ways when we first heared them." We stayed low and kep' quiet.

Five men come over the rise, but it was the first one, with the torch, that caught my attention. He was a big brute, over six feet, and had a patch over his left eye. Keith Blalock! From their talk we knowed the others was Yankees. Then, right in front a us, Blalock stopped short and shushed the Yanks.

He stood there fer a long time, his good eye measurin' every tree on the scarp; not a word was spoke. Then, outa the stillness he said slow and evenlike, "Step onto the road where a man can see who's watchin' him." He directed his words at the whole piney grove, but we was convinced he knowed exactly where we laid. When a feller has scouted as long as that one has, he can jes sense the eyes of any man or beast, no matter where they be.

So we stepped out, and George come up close behind us. We warn't afeared a nothin' 'cause the Yanks had nary a gun amongst them, and we was double armed.

Now Blalock sized that up real quick too, so he sets hisself on a log stump and commences to tell how pretty the night was, even iffen it was a might cold. I was surprised at how soft he spoke, and how mannerly he was, tho' he did have a wild look in his eye. Some folkses say we all carried that look during the outlier times.

Afore long, he offered us some brandy, which we accepted, and the jug was passed all around. Then he got down to business. He asked iffen we cared to join them and go over to the Tenth Michigan Regiment encamped in Tennessee.

Well, we was sick a army life and had not a bit a use fer it no more. Iffen we was forced to join a reg'lar regiment agin, however, it would be on the side of General Robert E. Lee. We never said a thing a that to Keith Blalock tho', saw no need fer it. We jes thanked him fer the brandy and pronounced that we had places to be.

He never made no argument 'bout it atall, jes gathered up his Yankee friends and was gone.

That was the first and the onliest time I ever met Keith Blalock, but he shore come to be some kinda legend around this country.

We stayed 'bout a week nigh George's place, always sleepin' in a tiny cave up above the house. At night we all foraged 'bout the neighborhood fer food, a little a this and a little a that, to keep Celie and their youngun. I reckon you'd call it stealin', but we never gave it no mind then.

One night we tumbled onto a still-house, and that shore started us on a lark. I reckon we drunk a whole house full a liquor. Afore you knowed it we was singin' our way into Banner Elk. That was where we met the Captain.

'Twas early in February, and there was a big crowd a men there, all gathered 'bout Captain James. Champion was his name, a Yankee from Ohio or Indiana, one or t'other, a stocky man. He was gen'rally a recruiter fer the Thirteenth Tennessee, United States Army, but this time he was collectin' men fer a raid on the Home Guard at Camp Mast, which warn't far from Hettie's. We saw that most a the men with him was our own boys, scouters and outliers and all. We knowed some of them 'cause we scrounged 'bout with them.

Hell, right there in the twinkle of an eye we joined up. Never knowed why, 'cause we warn't no Yankee stooges. I reckon it seemed a good way to get even with the Guard. And I thought I might drop in on Hettie too. So off we went, 'bout one hundred a the sorriest bunch you ever seed. There was a few number twelve shotguns and hog rifles amongst us; some had no guns atall, jes sticks.

The Captain led us, or we him, to Valle Crucis, where we kilt one a Henry Taylor's beeves, cooked it, and had supper.

Then the Captain told ever'body that no looting would be tolerated, and we was there only to burn the camp and capture the Guard and their arms. Some several men fell out right then, 'cause they had only joined in the hopes of some plunder. The rest of us started down the road agin.

We crossed Brushy Fork Creek nigh Ben Councill's place, took the ridge above Cove Creek, and come down on the camp jes before dawn. The ground was friz solid, and our horses made so much clatter every dog in the world was awoked and yappin'. Then a flock a sheep scattered in front a us, every which way and down the ridge t'wards the camp, bells janglin' and sheep a-bleatin'. Hell's bells! Now, why the Guard never stirred I ain't never figured, but they slept on through. Champion, he had us spread out and build fires all over, so's to make us look like a big army.

Come the dawn all a rosy glow, the camp roused and looked out to discover they was surrounded! The Captain sent a man down under a truce flag to demand their surrender in half a hour.

Major Bingham warn't at the camp that night, so one a their other officers had a poll taken, and they voted, 'bout six to one, to surrender. What a wonder they had when it was discovered they was took in by a bunch a their own ragtag neighbors.

So off we went with our prisoners, two-by-two, with their blanket rolls over their shoulders, down Cove Creek, acrost the Watauga River and over the Beech Mountain. In all the excitement I forgot all 'bout Hettie.

At Banner Elk we divided up, George, me and Isaac marchin' with the ones taken to Lewis Banner's fer the night.

After ever'body fell asleep, several a the prisoners escaped. It warn't no matter to us, 'cause they was all paroled and turned loose the next day anyhow, 'cept fer near a dozen who had voted to not surrender. They was sent to a prison camp in Tennessee, which was bad, 'cause some a them died over there. One was Paul Farthing, who I remember was in the Watauga Minute Men when it was first organized way back in '61.

We took off too when the prisoners was free, back to George's place. When he told Celie all a our antics with the Captain, she got mad in a minute. Was s'mad she didn't know what to do, then she commenced to cuss like a sea horse. Cussed his head plumb off. She had a temper.

George said that was the maddest he ever seed Celie in his life, never seed her fit and scratch afore. Course, we all knowed she was in the right. We had no business gittin' drunk and goin' off into the dickens.

Well, Isaac and me left the two a them be, and they made up afore long. Fierce words needs mendin', Maw always told us that.

I still call to mind several other happenings from that February. One time we had gone into Yancey County to gather some store fer Celie, and we passed by a little house settin' in a wee holler under the old Black Dome.

We was half starved, so we commenced to scout surround the place. We opined that there was jes a old stooped widder woman livin' there, 'cause we saw her hangin' out some clothes and there was no trousers. She might be havin' company soon, fer there was several loaves a bread and a pie settin' in the window.

Whilst we was figurin' all this out, she took the vittles inside and shut the window. So then George come up with a scheme.

In the black a night we sneaked up and borrowed one a her dresses, all flowers and sech, and a big floppy bonnet. "Come mornin', " George said, " we will fix Isaac up in these and send him to her door as a decoy whilst we go to the back..."

"I ain't a-gonna' do no sech a thing nohow," complained Isaac. "You do it, Alf!"

"But I got this moustache, and you don't spect me to shave it off, do you? You are the youngest, so you can pass off better'n me or George."

"Shoot," he said, "why do I always git the dirty jobs? I ain't a-gonna' do it fer nothin'. We can jes put a gun to her and take what we want. What the hell's the diff'rence?"

George pointed out that Isaac wouldn't want nobody a pokin' a gun to our own maw's head, and it warn't right to treat the old lady thataway iffen there was a better plot. "Besides," said I, "she might have a gun herself, a-livin' all alone like this."

Well, come mornin', we set it up. First we had to beat the ice outa the dress cause it was stiff as a board. Even our own britches was friz so's you could feel the ice. When Isaac was finally in the frock, it was a bit short, so we hitched his pants up some. "What am I gonna say anyhow?" He was still a-fightin'. "What lame alibi has some *girl* fer roamin' 'bout here?"

"Calm down boy," George answered. "It don't matter what you say, jes so you keep her attention. "Now there," he was a-fixin' Isaac's bow. "Give us a minute or two afore you start out. Then jes call her to the outside."

79

So George and me skulked around behind, crouchin' low, 'cause with the trees all bare there warn't much cover. We got to gigglin' along the way tho', and kep' tryin' to shush each other.

Now, jes 'bout the time we approached the window, "WHAM" goes a shotgun, and then commenced the widder a-screechin' after Isaac. He was racing lickety-split acrost her frosty garden patch, holdin' his bonnet on his head, and his dress a-flappin' like tin along behind him.

She was either a poor shot or had no mind to put a hole in her own dress, fer Isaac made it free and clear. We managed to snatch a rooster and the apple pie afore she come back, cussin' like a drill sergeant.

Isaac was as mad as the widder when we catched up to him. "I told you I hadn't orta do sech a crazy thing! She warn't tricked fer a second, knowed it was her own clothes. Damn it boys, next time have somebody else be the fool." We liked to died laughin' as he tore at the dress tryin' to git out of it. Course, George had to add to his misery. "You orta keep the bonnet Isaac, it favors your color and makes your face light up."

Finally we got down to work on a genuine feast. We axed the head offen the rooster, watched it run around in circles a-lookin' fer it agin till it finally croaked, and then we soaked it in some hot water and commenced pluckin' feathers. This was woman's work, along with tearin' out the innards, and that was where Isaac drawed the line. Did enough woman's work fer one day he said, and we roared agin.

Even with all a that, it warn't half a the fun that night. When the meal was near ready, I went down to the creek to draw some water. I was no sooner stooped down when Isaac come a-yellin', "Bear! Bear! It's jes eatin' George up!" I grabbed m'gun and off we flew. The bear had treed George and we could hear it poppin' its teeth when we run up. Then it wheeled on us and I could see the shine a the fire in his eyes. In a thought or two it rose up on two legs and come t'ward us. I took quick aim and killed that gentleman deader'n four o'clock.

George had only a scratch or two, but the bear had ruint the pie and the chicken. We reckoned he musta been disturbed outa his den by some conscripts somewheres. The critter had sauntered in betwixt the boys and their guns. Isaac said when he went a-runnin' fer help, "'twas like a dream—I was a-dealin' m'feet and a-doin' no good." We laughed agin at that, and then made the best of ever'thing. Bear meat is coarse but it eats good iffen you're hungry.

Worst of all, we discovered the ruckus had scared our horses off. We never did find them, tho' we searched ever'where the next day. I reckon somebody else found them and took them off. Because a that, George decided he had better go back and see to his family. We was sorry to see him go, but we understood why. He asked us iffen we wanted to go with him but we declined. He had enough to care fer, and that neighborhood was 'bout cleaned out.

Isaac and me considered we might go into Madison County, 'cause we heared there was a place, the Laurel Valley, where the people was friendly and would feed the men. It seemed we was forever hungry. We always called that winter our "starvin' time."

* * *

3 March 1865
Shelton Laurel
Madison County, North Carolina

Dear Maw and Paw,

We ain't been bothered by nobody ever since we arrived in the Shelton Laurel. This section is almost all solid fer the Union, and them that ain't just mind their own business. We spend most a the daylight in a little shack we built up a creek called Hickory Fork. We call it our Devil's Den. We are learnin' to make ourselves do lotsa things we never did think we could do.

It's a strange place here fer us tho', and we hunger fer ever'body at home. You are always on our minds.

The hardest thing is that we don't belong nowhere. Iffen we was to fight fer the South, how long could we live? And if we joined the Yanks hereabout, we knowed our dreams would haunt us. So we jes keep a-goin', fast and loose, and a-wanderin' lonely.

Sometimes in the cold stillness betwixt the dark and daylight, Isaac and me will git to mopin' 'bout the good old times.

It was sech pleasure when we was little boys to tromp acrost the fields and up the holler to Aunt Fanny and Uncle Squire's house, a-thinkin' the world's a wonderful place to live in. She might be out churnin' milk in a piggin, or inside mendin' clothes, but when she saw us a-comin' she would smile like a star that fell from heaven and smother us with sweetness. She always had a biscuit fer us, and our eyes jes shone when she covered it with blackberry jam or sourwood honey. Then she would scoot us outside to play with Silas and Carroll.

Afterwards on the way home, Isaac would try and jump the creek, every time, and I don't reckon he ever managed it. You always wondered why he was so wet. I thought he wouldn't have no sense if he met it comin' down the road.

We couldn't count the Saturdays we went there after our chores was done, in the sunshine or rain.

Now, since I quit the army and the way things are, I wonder if Aunt Fanny would still be so happy to see us.

There is rumors all over here that the war is all but over, and we think it might be true. So we aim to repair back home as soon as this letter is posted, and we hope to find ever'body well there. It's near fifty miles and will take us awhile fer we lost our horses.

We are both doin' fine and will have many things to report, but one thing happened yesterday I have to narrate to you right now.

Afore sunrise, we was headin' to the creek to try our luck at fishin'; we had just crossed a trail when we heared the queerest noise, a sort of tinkle like a bell or something.

In jes a moment, here come maybe eight or nine Indians all surround a Yankee prisoner. They was Cherokees from the Qualla Reservation I reckon, but two of them was dressed in Confederate uniforms. They had on silver earrings and bells, and one wore a feathered headband. We spect he was the leader. They was 'bout forty yards off when they stopped and forced the poor Yank to his knees.

Lord, the next thing we knowed, they scalped him alive. They jes took a knife and made a cut, and then tore the rest of it off. Then the one with the feathers hung it on his gun. They stabbed him once and stripped off his uniform and left him there to die. Isaac was sick over it and I don't blame him, although I reckon I have seed worse things. We went to him after they left, but he had breathed his last. We buried him the best we could under some rocks.

Wild Indians shore do put a fright into a man. I would heap ruther be shot by a bullet than have some savage a-choppin' at my head, trying to axe my scalp off fer a damn trophy.

Well, that is our story.

We will tell you more when we return home. Paw, we will do all a the spring plowing fer you, and be glad of it.

Your loving sons,
Isaac and Alf

* * *

The way back to Watauga was easy goin', tho' we like to friz to death up on the heights. At times we feared to sleep lest the fire would go out, so we kep' awake a-tellin' a haints and headless men walkin' 'bout in the dark.

At least nobody bothered us along the way, and we was careful a that. One man in Mitchell County had a wagon and he give us a ride fer near ten miles and his wife give us a sack a food, too. They told us ever'thing in Watauga was the same as when we left. We was sorely disappointed to hear that, but we shoulda supposed it I reckon. We was only gone 'bout six weeks.

When we reached home, the folkses was jes s'proud to have our family t'gether agin. The first evenin' we took down the Sacred Harp book and ever'body sang, and Paw read several verses from the Bible.

There was *some* little difference in the wind surround Watauga I noticed. All the Union people was now goin' 'bout all biggety whilst the Confederates was not nearly so bold. And I don't recall the Guard visiting us one time after we returned.

I took off to see Hettie as often as I could. We spent them days strolling 'bout here and there when the weather was nice, but never on the roads.

There was one time we was hiking, the twenty-eighth a March, a day I will never ferget. 'Twas a fair mornin' and I was at her place early, even afore they was up from the table. Her maw begged me to set and tell all 'bout our adventure in Madison, but Hettie hauled me away afore I had time even fer "iffen you please." Said she wanted to go up to Howard's Knob above Boone. I knowed better than to argue, but that was a far piece and would take the whole mornin'.

"I want t'find me some pink lady slippers," she said, kinda honeylike and all soft talk. I commenced to ask iffen they warn't any of them planted somewheres closer to home, but I held m'tongue, and off we went along the Rich Mountain path. Several times along the way I pointed at some flower or t'other but she would pay them no mind, and when I held her hand or kissed her I felt as if she was off in another world. Finally, whilst we was a-restin' in a swag down from the knob, she spit it out. "Alf, I missed m'time."

"I don't know what time it is," I said, a tad mistook. "Ain't noon yet I don't reckon."

"I mean m'time a the month! I missed it, Alf."

Now I always was kinda slow on woman folk things, and it took her several more stabs afore it stuck. Finally the dawn did break on me, but 'xactly the same time some awful racket come from down below, a-bouncin' acrost the hollers. I thought fer a moment it was my brain come to life, till I remembered that sound. It was gunfire!

We hid out and watched the most severe thing. The Yankees was attacking Boone! They had come down the road from Hodges Gap when some a the new Home Guard that was gatherin' spotted them and opened fire, and then all hell broke loose. At first it looked like jes a small force, tho' we learn't later there was near six thousand Yankee horsemen all told. It didn't take but the first a them to make short work a the Guard.

After all we been through, and jes whilst I was thinkin' it might end any day, here comes the war straight to my own home. It was one thing when we tore up Camp Mast, but a Yankee army! Yes, some several home Yankees from the mountains was in it, yet this was a Yankee army fer a fact. Oh, Lord, what a fear I had, jes went stiff when they come pourin' in a-blazin' away at the whole town.

We was too high and far to see it all, but we heared later how poor Jacob Councill was a-ploughin' his field and went runnin' to git his horse to the barn when he was shot dead. Ephraim Norris was kilt and my own Uncle Warren Green, one a Maw's brothers, was too.

The Yankees chased Calvin Green through town, and he blasted a arm off one a them afore they wounded him and left him fer dead. One lady with a baby in her arms come out on her porch when the ruckus commenced and several shots tore up the door frame on both sides a her head afore she made it back inside. Several others was wounded and then they burnt the jail down.

We could see the fire and smell the smoke, and all a sudden I jes could not take it no more. You live fer years under strains of all kinds and fear and killin', and there comes a time when you jes cain't take it no more. I let loose a holler like some crazy man and, with Hettie a-pullin' aginst m'arm, picked up a huge rock and hurled it with all a m'strength down the hill. The helpless thing flew only 'bout ten feet when it hit a boulder and broke up into a thousand pieces.

Then I did it agin, and agin, till a little sharp piece a rock bounced up and struck Hettie on the forehead. When the blood come s'bad it made me feel as iffen all a my own lifeblood was a-drainin' outa me, and I had to set down. Hettie could only stare at me in wonder. Warn't till some several minutes after the whole thing ended I come to m'senses. I dabbed a little at Hettie's forehead, tied m'handkerchief over it, and then took her home fast.

Nary 'nother word was said the whole way 'bout the news she had been tryin' to give me. I got her to home and warned her Maw, then I lit out to tell Paw that the Yankees was here.

By the time I made it home it looked as iffen the trouble was over, fer soon after the battle the enemy headed east t'wards Wilkesboro. We all felt relieved.

But then, afore another week was up, their general, name was Stoneman, sent more soldiers into Boone to guard his rear. The one in charge a this was Colonel George Kirk, and that man shore had a special spite fer the people here in the mountains.

He barricaded our Meat Camp Road and some othern, and fortified the courthouse in town, cuttin' gun holes in it. Kirk made his headquarters at Councill's house, where his men jes ruint the fencing and tromped the yard bare, covering it with beef hides and chicken feathers and putrid meat. They pissed all over the place any time they pleased.

They was ransackin' houses all around fer food, so we did what we could to keep our property safe, even took the hams out to the pasture and placed them on big rocks and camouflaged them with moss. We had our guns ready too, but iffen they came, I knowed they would have their own way.

Paw insisted that iffen trouble did come I was to take the children up on the mountain and the Yanks could have whatever food they found. Then he had me take the cows up on the Little Cavit on Rich Mountain where they might be safe. Some other neighbors had their cows hid up there too, and I couldn't help but think on the people we stole from. I moved the cows in the second week a April. I recall the time 'cause I was on my way back home when I seed the corpse.

The remains of a human body had been shoved into the cavity of a blowed down oak tree. It was all covered with brush and leaves, 'cept the head, fer I seed the white hair showin' through. It stopped me in m'tracks. As I poked 'bout I spied a hickory thong nearby, dangling from a white oak, with a noose still on it! I puzzled over it fer some time afore I went on my way.

I told the folkses about it but they had no idea who the corpse could be. All night long it kep' a-hauntin' me, and the next day I was drawed back to the same spot. This time as I come near I heared someone a-sobbin'. I crept closer, and there was a woman, standin' at the root a the tree with the skull in her apron, cryin' as iffen her heart would break. At the sight a that my eyes watered up, and I thought fer a moment that maybe I still had some heart after all. I went up to her but there was no consoling. She said it was her husband—Tom Stout! I recalled the story Hettie and her maw told me, how the Home Guard had snatched him off on account a the crimes his sons had done. They hung him! What is it the preachers say 'bout the sins a the fathers passin' on to the sons? Here it was the other way 'bout, and now the mother was payin' fer the deeds too. She lived over the line, in Ashe County, name was Elizabeth she said, and somebody had told her where her husband's body could be found.

A scene sech as that can fire direct into your soul. I reckon every'body has times, and they don't know why, when a thing will happen and you learn somethin'. Well, that was the time I learnt t'stop feelin' sorry fer m'self. And I don't believe I have done a bit much of it since. I had knowed all along that *ever'body* was sufferin', but when you git unnerved like that, and you don't feel good, then you *understand* it. Yes, sir!

It was only a few days after that, early in the evenin', whilst me and Paw was fussin' over some fence the Yanks had made off with, when all a sudden Allen come a-runnin' down the lane. "It's over! The war's over! *The war is over!*"

At first we wondered where he got the news from, not willin' to trust a boy, but he was convincing. "The word is flyin' all through the hills, Paw. Go on up yonder by the road and you'll see!"

Allen was right. The war was over. Finally! General Lee had surrendered the army at Appomattox. We all cheered and cried and carried on most a the night. I think Maw even had a little drink that time.

When I was finally in bed and ever'thing was quiet, and I couldn't sleep , I tried to picture the boys, my old comrades, layin' down their guns and our battle flag, but I couldn't do it.

Later on I read where a Federal general said there was "an awed stillness" on the field, "and breath-holding, as if it were the passing of the dead." I discovered there was jes nine soldiers left in our Company E to surrender the last arms a the Watauga Minute Men, and only two a them had signed up with me at the very beginning, Cicero Harmon and Joseph Howington. But several other'ns from Watauga who joined the company in '62 also come through at the end, James Coffey and Bill Foster and Wellington Adams, who is brother Allen's father-in-law now.

It was queer, but somehow I sorta wisht I had been there at the end too. Iffen I had, then maybe I woulda felt more like tellin' 'bout the war to the children, instead a keepin' things to m'self s'much. Anyway, it was over, and we celebrated as iffen the weight a the world was lifted.

Course I spected ever'thing to finally be quiet and peaceful, but it warn't thataway atall. Fer months and months the county was infested with all sorts a roving characters and desperadoes. The worst a them was led by Wade and Simmons, two worthless Yankees who deserted Stoneman's command and joined up with some a our own bushwackers to plunder the neighborhoods, takin' advantage of all the confusion after the war. They went ridin' up to a house with guns pointed, threatenin' to shoot iffen anybody opened their mouths, whilst they searched through drawers and boxes and took what they fancied. Why, one time they seed a little child playin' on a fence whilst the mother was a-workin' in her field, and they commenced to take target practice till finally one a their rifle balls struck the poor child dead.

On and on it went till finally the Federal government formed some a the old Confederate officers into a new Home Guard to protect the citizens. Colonel Joe Todd was made the captain a that, and order was restored right quick. Most a the misery come to a end an ever'body got on with jes plain livin' onest agin.

The first thing Hettie and me done was to git married. We made it jes a plain thing, and I was happy fer that. Didn't have nothin' to make it fancy with nohow. Paw give us a grand present tho', a piece of land in the line of Nettle Knob, up the road from the Baptist Church of Christ nigh Howard's Creek. I reckon it was the land he had in mind fer Adam.

Me and Hettie built our fences, and ploughed the fields and planted seeds. Then the years jes rolled on and on.

We had some several children, eight a them in all, and soon the birthdays followed, one after t'other, faster and faster. They say time is mostly measured by births and marriages and deaths. But to me it sometimes jes disappears, like the mornin' clouds, that drift up outa the mountains t'ward heaven.

I onest heared a man claim that those of us who was soldiers learnt how to "value" life. Hell, I learnt that you live as long as you can and die when you cain't help it.

I knowed bad times, I shorely did, but shoot, it's a long road that never has no turns. And there was goodness too, I swear, and good and bad people too. I remember them.

Ain't never seed George Patrick agin after the war. Jes lost him I reckon. He might have moved away from the mountains. Me, I never left no more in my whole life.

Keith and Malinda Blalock has a family now and still live under the Grandfather. I heared he murdered John Boyd nearly a year after the war 'cause Boyd took some part in killin' Keith's stepfather, but nothin' come of it, and they say he is a respectable citizen over there now.

Adam's widow married Reubin Isaacs and moved away. Whereat I don't know.

M'brothers and sisters all was married and had families, tho' many a them are gone now. . . . Celia, and Joe when he was only thirty. And dear Isaac, he farmed the piece nigh to me, he was only thirty-eight when he died.

And cousin Silas, and Carroll . . .

But they are all still with me in my mind. Sometimes I think my only bright memories are from long ago. My childhood friends and the ones I mourn jes gathers around agin.

Maw passed on in 1886. It's hard on a boy when his mother goes, and it don't matter none how old he is neither. You know that' s forever, and she will never be able t'speak to you agin.

And my darlin' Hettie, she died way too soon. Was in the best part a her life, only forty-four, and she never even got to hold no grandchild.

I always was sorry she had sech a scrape-along journey with me, but I reckon she would jes say "Never you mind with it."

I cain't hardly recollect the funeral preachin' no more, don't believe I heared it. She died in this house on the second day a March, 1890. We carried her up to the cemetery on the hilltop, and my, there was a lotsa people come. The wind was a-blowin' awful cold that day, too.

'Twas only two months after that when Paw went, and we laid him in the Meat Camp Church ground aside of Maw. I remember Paw's estate sale so clear. Brother Allen was in charge a that. I bought four sheep, some corn, a yellow blanket, two pairs a socks, a milk pitcher, and a set of glass tumblers. Hettie had always loved them tumblers so. Sister Sally bought the Bible. I often wisht I had got that to pass on down to the children.

Along' bout then I had m'stroke, and what they call the Bright's disease commenced. But you jes keep on a-goin'. Used t'be I was s'stout, could work a day and a half with no rest. I would ruther work as to play any time. There's a kinda sadness in studyin' back over where you been...and all what you did.

I ain't always done right in this whole lifetime, I know it. Tho' the sinner in me bloom agin, I can be peaceful inside, 'cause I have lived the best I knowed how.

The moon is beaming. I reckon the boys will be a-comin' in from the barn soon. Maybe I'll close my eyes fer a little while.

Alford and Hettie's children were:

1. Roby Carroll, b. Oct. 1865, married first Martha Jane Beach, and second Nettie Ashley. Roby and Martha had Lucy Emma, 1890; Allen, 1892; Hettie, 1894; Effie Mae, 1897; and Virginia Edna, 1899. Roby and Nettie had Nora, 1900; Daisy, 1905; Boyd, 1906; Ida, 1907; Vinnie, 1908; and Bina, 1914.

2. Susie Emma, b. 1868, married William Alan Pennell, and had Josie Geneva, 1895.

3. Martha Jane, b. 1870, married John Penley, and had Carter Daniel, 1891; William Eddie, ca. 1892; B. Letha, 1893; Robert Pinkney, 1895; Blanche Lettie, 1898; Della Elizabeth, 1900; Julie, 1902; Bertha Arvilla, 1905; Lillie Marie, 1907; Edna Lena, 1909; and Arlie Albert, 1912.

4. Mary, b. 1874, married William Isaacs, and had Rhoda, 1897; Dora, 1899; Spencer; Allie; and probably others. They moved to Tennessee.

5. William Henry, b. 1875, married Lura Inez Barnes, and had Alice Inez, 1898; Ella Lavonia, 1901; and twins John Alfred and George Lee, 1904.

6. Arthur Hardin, b. 1877, married Naomi Isabel Bumgarner, and had Rebecca Magdalena, 1902; Claude James, 1904; Gurney Rom, 1905; Texie Mae, 1907; Mary Lee, 1909; Wilburn Roscoe, 1911; Floy, 1914, who died young; Ruby Clare, 1917; Simon Alfred, 1919; Mamie Carol, 1921; Blanco McKinley, 1923; and Bernard Hardin, 1927. (Claude James, above, is the author's father.)

7. Nelia Cordelia, b. 1882, married John Allen Beach, and had Willy Frances, who died young; Silas Clay, who died young; Lola May, 1908; Bertie Faye, 1910; Ralph Upton, 1912; Grace, 1914, who died young; Bass Britten, who died young; Mary Isabell, 1918; and Mable Irene, 1921, who died young.

8. Maggie, born 1886, married David Isaacs, and had Stewart; Jackie; Billie Joe; and others. They moved to Tennessee.

BIBLIOGRAPHY

Books:

Alexander, Nancy T. *Here Will I Dwell: The Story of Caldwell County, North Carolina*. Lenoir: 1956.

Army of the Confederate States. *Army Regulations*. Richmond: West & Johnston, 1861.

Arthur, John P. *History of Watauga County, North Carolina*. Reprint of 1915 edition. Easley: Southern Historical Press, 1976.

Bailey, Ronald H. *Forward to Richmond*. Alexandria: Time-Life Books, 1983.

Barrett, John G. *The Civil War in North Carolina*. Chapel Hill: The University of North Carolina Press, 1963.

Billings, John D. *Hard-Tack and Coffee: The Unwritten Story of Army Life*. Boston: George M. Smith, 1887.

Blackmun, Ora. *Western North Carolina: Its Mountains and Its People to 1880*. Boone: Appalachian Consortium Press, 1977.

Buchanan, Lamont. *A Pictorial History of the Confederacy*. New York: Bonanza Books, 1951.

Bull, Rice C. *Soldiering: The Civil War Diary of Rice C. Bull*. Edited by K. Jack Bauer. Novato: Presidio Press, 1977.

Campbell, John C. *The Southern Highlander & His Homeland*. Lexington: The University Press of Kentucky, 1969.

Catton, Bruce. *The American Heritage Picture History of the Civil War*. New York: American Heritage/Bonanza Books, 1982.

Catton, Bruce. *Gettysburg: The Final Fury*. Garden City: Doubleday & Co., 1974.

Chaitin, Peter M. *The Coastal War*. Alexandria: Time-Life Books, 1984.

Channing, Steven A. *Confederate Ordeal*. Alexandria: Time-Life Books, 1984.

Clark, Champ. *Gettysburg*. Alexandria: Time-Life Books, 1985.

Coddington, Edwin B. *The Gettysburg Campaign*. Reprint of Morningside Bookshop 1979 edition. New York: Charles Scribner's Sons, 1984.

Davis, Burke. *The Civil War: Strange & Fascinating Facts*. New York: The Fairfax Press, 1982.

Davis, William C. *Brother Against Brother*. Alexandria: Time-Life Books, 1983.

Davis, William C. *Death In The Trenches*. Alexandria: Time-Life Books, 1986.

Dugger, Shepherd M. *The Balsam Groves of the Grandfather Mountain*. Reprint of 1934 edition. Banner Elk: The Puddingstone Press, 1974.

Dugger, Shepherd M. *The War Trails of the Blue Ridge*. Reprint of 1932 edition. Banner Elk: The Puddingstone Press, 1974.

Fink, Paul. *Bits of Mountain Speech*. Boone: The Appalachian Consortium, 1974.

Foote, Shelby. *The Civil War: A Narrative*. 3 vols. New York: Random House, 1958-74.

Goolrick, William K. *Rebels Resurgent*. Alexandria: Time-Life Books, 1985.

Hall, Joseph S. *Smokey Mountain Folks and Their Lore.* Asheville: Gilbert Printing Co., 1960.

Hansen, Harry. *The Civil War.* New York: Bonanza Books, 1962.

Hassler, William W. *A. P. Hill: Lee's Forgotten General.* Chapel Hill: The University of North Carolina Press, 1984.

Jaynes, Gregory. *The Killing Ground.* Alexandria: Time-Life Books, 1986.

Johnson, Curt, and McLaughlin, Mark. *Civil War Battles.* New York: Fairfax Press, 1981.

Jordan, Weymouth T., ed. *North Carolina Troops 1861-1865 A Roster.* Vol. 9. Raleigh: Division of Archives and History, 1983.

Korn, Jerry. *Pursuit to Appomattox.* Alexandria: Time-Life Books, 1987.

Morley, Margaret W. *The Carolina Mountains.* Boston: Houghton Mifflin, 1913.

Newton, John, and Simons, Gerald, eds. *Lee Takes Command.* Alexandria: Time-Life Books, 1984.

Parris, John. *Roaming the Mountains.* Asheville: Citizen-Times Publishing Co., 1955.

Richardson, Ethel P., ed. *American Mountain Songs.* Greenberg Publisher, 1927.

Robertson, James I., Jr. *The Concise Illustrated History of the Civil War.* Harrisburg: National Historical Society, 1979.

Robertson, James I., Jr. *Tenting Tonight.* Alexandria: Time-Life Books, 1984.

Scott, W. W. *Annals of Caldwell County, North Carolina.* Lenoir: News Topic Printers, 1924.

Symonds, Craig L. *A Battlefield Atlas of the Civil War.* Baltimore: Nautical and Aviation Publishing Co. of America, 1983.

Tucker, Glenn. *Front Rank: The Story of North Carolina in the CivilWar*. Raleigh: Confederate Centennial Commission, 1962.

United States War Department. *War of the Rebellion: A Compilation of the Official Records of the Union and Confederate Armies*. Vols. 1-70. Washington: Government Printing Office, 1880-1901.

Van Noppen, Ina W. *Stoneman's Last Raid*. Raleigh: North Carolina State College Print Shop, 1961.

Walton, Col. Thomas G. *Sketches of the Pioneers in Burke County History*. Reprint of articles first published in Morganton Herald ca. 1894. Easley: Southern Historical Press, 1984.

Wigginton, Eliot, ed. *Foxfire*. Vols. 1-6. Garden City: Anchor Press/Doubleday, 1972-1980.

Wiley, Bell I. *The Life of Johnny Reb*. Baton Rouge: Louisiana State University Press, 1978.

Papers, letters, diaries, and other sources:

Duke University Manuscript Division.
Alfred Adams letter, 1862. William E. Ardrey diary, 1863-1864. William Byrnes diary and letters. William Chunn papers, 1861-1864. William F. Loftin collection. Joseph Overcash letters. Miscellaneous letters.

University of North Carolina Southern Historical Collection.
Cullen A. Battle papers. Berry G. Benson letter, 1863. George P. Erwin letter. Sam Furebaugh diary. George W. F. Harper diary. Edmund W. Jones letters. Miscellaneous Confederate papers.